THE CLUELESS ASPIRANT

PRANJAL HAZARIKA

Srishti
Publishers & Distributors

Srishti Publishers & Distributors
A unit of AJR Publishing LLP
212A, Peacock Lane
Shahpur Jat, New Delhi – 110 049

editorial@srishtipublishers.com

First Published by Srishti Publishers & Distributors in 2026

10 9 8 7 6 5 4 3 2 1

Dedicated to All the Civil Service Aspirants!
Those who made it and those who didn't!

Foreword

After the release of his impressive debut collection of short stories, *Fireflies in the Backyard,* in 2019, *The Clueless Aspirant* marks Pranjal Hazarika's foray into the world of storytelling in the longer format. Through this book, he aptly captures the microcosm of UPSC aspirants and the path of struggle and hardships that lies therein, which often goes unnoticed or unacknowledged. Hazarika doesn't keep that microcosm limited to just the preparation or passing of the exam; instead, he seamlessly intertwines the professional and personal lives of the protagonists. Hazarika takes the readers on a rollercoaster ride of relationships, love, heartbreak, hardships, perseverance, and self-introspection. The emotional and psychological journey of Civil Services aspirants is laid bare as the protagonists navigate the challenges of life, thereby allowing readers to feel a sense of familiarity with them.

The Clueless Aspirant is a deeply immersive and sensitively written narrative that captures the unadorned reality of one of India's most demanding journeys—the pursuit of the Civil Services Examination. Pranjal Hazarika writes not merely as a storyteller but as a keen observer of human ambition, vulnerability, and resilience. His prose is grounded, accessible, and unpretentious, allowing the story to flow naturally without literary excess, while still carrying emotional depth and authenticity.

The author's writing style is marked by clarity and realism. Scenes unfold with cinematic detail—be it the crowded lanes of Old Rajendra Nagar, the claustrophobic rental rooms of aspirants, the charged atmosphere of coaching classrooms, or the quiet introspection of late-night study sessions. The coaching ecosystem, peer competition, property dealers, group studies, mock tests, and superstition surrounding the exam are portrayed without judgment, but with sharp insight. Dialogue feels organic and regionally rooted, reflecting the diverse backgrounds of aspirants drawn from across India.

At its heart, this novel is not about success or failure alone—it is about the process. Through the journey of Samar Sarma, the author explores the psychological terrain of an aspirant: hope, self-doubt, distraction, jealousy, motivation, discipline, and emotional conflict. Samar is not idealised; he is flawed, hesitant, and often overwhelmed—making him deeply relatable. His struggles mirror those of countless young men and women who arrive in Delhi carrying dreams larger than their means.

The emotional core of the story lies in the delicate balance between aspiration and attachment. The evolving relationship between Samar and Abha is portrayed with nuance and restraint. Rather than romanticising it, the author presents love as both refuge and risk—capable of offering strength, yet equally capable of derailing focus in a high-stakes competitive environment. This emotional realism elevates the novel beyond a mere "exam story" into a broader commentary on youth, choice, and sacrifice.

After Samar manages to make it into the Civils, the story moves further to the daily life of a civil servant, something which has been barely documented in other similar works. The author's brilliance is evident in depicting the nuances of an arranged marriage, the expectations of a newlywed Jyotsna and her frustrations. I must appreciate the storytelling skills of the author to cover both the professional and personal life of a Civil servant in a fast-paced, simple yet engrossing narrative.

What sets *The Clueless Aspirant* apart is its honesty. I have been associated with the journey of the examination, and I can vouch for the authenticity and honesty with which Hazarika draws the inner worlds of his characters and the varied places and precarious situations that life takes them to. The author does not offer shortcuts, grand triumphs, or exaggerated heroism. Instead, he documents small victories, quiet failures, and gradual self-awareness. He makes us believe that hope and determination are essential in coping with the demands that life makes on us.

I am certain that this book will resonate strongly with civil services aspirants, former aspirants, and anyone who has chased a demanding dream under uncertain circumstances. It will also relate to womenfolk who have to continuously find a footing in a male-dominated society and the familial pressures they have to endure on a daily basis.

The Clueless Aspirant is, ultimately, a story about growing up—about learning that ambition requires discipline, that emotions demand balance, and the human ability to see positivity in any situation or phase of life.

I will sign off by offering my best wishes to both the author and the Publisher.

Piyush Arun Rohankar,
Author and Civil Servant

Acknowledgements

As I was a day scholar during my graduation, post-graduation, and PhD phase (from the University of Delhi), I always felt that I missed the fun and the experiences that hostel scholars get to live, experience, and learn from the outside world.

When I was preparing for the Civil Services, I shared rooms with the other aspirants for a few months to undertake the IAS coaching classes in Rajender Nagar and in Mukherjee Nagar (some of them have become good friends over the years, significantly, Pranav Ganesh, Salil Hasabnis, Sanjeev Sharma, Vivek Agarwal, Karamvir Chahar). I consider those rented accommodation days as my 'Hostel days', which I cherish to this day.

Rajender Nagar still gives me the goosebumps whenever I happen to pass through, even to this day, as it makes me nostalgic about those UPSC preparation days, walking every evening to the coaching classes, lengthy discussions on current topics and varied opinions of other aspirants, a few relaxing moments like watching late evening movies....

I used to wonder whether, if I manage to clear the UPSC Civil Services, a few years down the line, I will pen down those experiences and some events I witnessed among fellow aspirants...

So, finally, I decided to pen down those experiences in a book. There are very few books that tell the story of the UPSC days of aspirants: the struggle, the dedication, the efforts, the hardships, the pain, the heartbreak, the failure and sheer dejection, the joy and celebration...

Therefore, I am much obliged to Arup Bose for believing in me and letting me bring this journey of countless UPSC Aspirants to life in the form of a story. I sincerely acknowledge Stuti and the Srishti team for moulding the raw manuscript into a smooth version. A sincere thanks to Dipti Patel, WordFamous Literary Agency, for all her help.

I will always be grateful to Srishti Publishers for allowing me to connect with unknown readers through this book, my first novel, so they can get an insight into the UPSC Civil Services during preparation and into the professional life after clearing the coveted exam.

And lastly, I hope this book reaches all the countless UPSC Civil Service Aspirants!

CHAPTER 1

The Brahmaputra Mail finally arrived at the platform of the Old Delhi Railway Station late in the evening, moving at a crawling pace after a few halts through the outskirts of Delhi. Samar was one of the last passengers to deboard the second-class compartment. His head was spinning, and his body felt dizzy and unsteady, as if he were still in motion. Samar had boarded the Brahmaputra Mail from Guwahati, and he was to stay for a few days in Dwarka with a distant cousin, Atul, and his wife, Meenu, who lived in a rented apartment in Sector 10.

Outside the main entrance of the station, the scene was chaotic. Everyone seemed to be in a hurry, trying to get somewhere. Men were pulling their luggage, women were struggling with their children, and coolies expertly balanced multiple loads, as if preparing for the civil services exam, while auto-rickshaw and taxi drivers competed fiercely for potential passengers.

"Hello… Oh, hello, *Bhaiya! Kahan Jaana Hain*? Auto *chahiye*?" a middle-aged Sardarji shouted at Samar.

"Dwarka, Sector 10," he answered.

"Three hundred rupees," said the Sardarji.

"No, no, that is too much. I will pay by the metre," Samar insisted.

"Three hundred rupees is not much. It is the right price," the Sardarji countered.

"I will go only if you use the metre; otherwise, I will look for someone else," Samar said firmly.

"*Accha*! Accha! Okay, as you insist! Here, give me your luggage, *Sirji*!"

The Sardarji placed Samar's suitcase on the floor of the auto. Samar hopped in, and the Sardarji kick-started the rickety black and yellow auto. He manoeuvred expertly through buses, taxis, cars, rickshaws, and tempos in the crowded streets. It took about an hour and a half to reach Samar's cousin's place in Dwarka. Samar paid 240 rupees based on the metre reading and was glad he had insisted on the metre rather than a flat charge. Being dependent on his elder brother for expenses, he needed to avoid unnecessary ones.

After dinner with Atul and his wife, Samar collapsed on the makeshift bed in the living room, utterly exhausted.

Samar had arrived a week before the commencement of civil services coaching classes at Rajan's IAS Study Circle in Delhi. It was the first week of September 2000, and the weather in Delhi was pleasantly mild. The blistering heat of May to July was over, and the harsh winter was yet to set in.

Samar hailed from Guwahati, where he shared an ancestral family home with his elder brother, Amar, his sister-in-law, Maloti, and his nephew, Abhimanyu. Amar, who was much older than Samar, had a low-paying clerical job in the state government secretariat. Samar had lost his mother when he was young, and a few years later, his father passed away. After his father's death, his sister-in-law became more assertive in the household. She had little affection for Samar. She wanted him to find a job and contribute to the household income. However, Amar encouraged him to pursue a career of his own choosing. Though Maloti did not support this, she had to abide by Amar's wishes, which sometimes led to occasional arguments between them. During his graduation days, Samar took on tutoring neighbouring school students to cover his additional expenses.

Samar was in Delhi to prepare for the civil services. Since his late teenage years, he harboured aspirations to become an IAS officer. His ambition had ignited when, in his eleventh grade, he stumbled upon a magazine called *The Competition Success Review*, which featured an IAS topper on its front cover. The interview with the topper inspired him, painting a picture of the respect and reputation in society that came with the service. Maloti often mocked his dreams, but Samar vowed to prove his worth one day.

Very few candidates from Assam succeeded in the UPSC examinations, and Samar hardly knew anyone who had. However, he fortuitously chanced upon a distant relative who was preparing for the exams during his second year of college. The relative advised him to refer to the NCERT textbooks from grades IX-XII and join Rajan's coaching in Delhi. Once he graduated, Samar planned to move to Delhi to begin preparing for the civil services exams.

***

The next day, Samar visited Rajan's IAS Study Circle in Old Rajendra Nagar to inquire about admissions. The Old Rajendra Nagar area was a typical locality in Central Delhi. It appeared to have been planned several decades ago, when not every household owned a vehicle. Today, the streets were cluttered with haphazardly parked cars, tempos, autos, scooters, and cycle rickshaws jostling for every inch of space. The scene was an eyesore for any city planner, but who cared? Prominent bank branches, ATMs, property dealers, departmental stores, juice corners, eateries, budget hotels, beauty parlours, small business shops, photostat centres, and stationery shops all lined the bustling commercial lane. From the latest issue of *The Competition Success Review,* Sorabh Babu, the latest IAS topper, seemed to beckon to Samar with a half-smiling face, as if to say, "Beat me if you can!"

It was an easy task to locate Rajan's IAS Study Circle, situated on the first floor of a commercial building. There was a flurry of activity around the building, with many young men and women, likely civil services aspirants, arriving individually or with relatives. Someone directed Samar to Elangovan, the manager of the study circle. Other civil services aspirants had gathered in a small waiting area outside Elangovan's chamber. Enlarged photos of successful candidates from recent years adorned a 4 x 5 ft notice board in the narrow corridor. The images were low-resolution, likely enlarged from passport-sized original photos. The board proudly displayed the caption, "11 Successful IAS Candidates in the Last Civil Services Exam" in bold letters.

"Will my photo make it someday?" Samar wondered, feeling as though the successful IAS toppers' faces were mocking him.

Forty minutes later, Samar finally met Elangovan. A typical middle-aged Tamilian with accented Hindi, Elangovan had a wheatish complexion. The way aspirants waited for him showed that he was an important functionary at the institute.

"Sir, I am Samar. Samar Sarma," he introduced himself.

"Okay. Good," Elangovan replied.

"How much is the course fee, Sir?" Samar asked.

"The fee is Rs. 23,000 for General Studies. Admissions begin in three days. Anything else?"

Samar wanted to seek more information, but Elangovan's body language was not encouraging enough."IAS topper *banna hain*!" a short, loudly dressed man called out as Samar descended the stairs. He handed Samar a card, introducing himself as a representative of Talwar Properties, a local property dealer.

"Admission *chahiye*! Room *toh chahiye hoga!"* he exclaimed.

Samar nodded, wishing to move to Old Rajendra Nagar before classes began.

"*Toh chalo mere saath. Aapko ek se ek* special room *dekhata hoon,*" said the short fellow.

Samar climbed onto his rickety scooter, and they headed to Talwar Properties' office. The ride was quite bumpy due to several potholes in the road, and Samar heaved a sigh of relief when the scooter finally came to a halt in front of the dealer's office, just two streets away from the institute.

The short man ushered Samar into an 8x10 ft chamber. Vinay Talwar, a young Punjabi fellow, sat flipping through the pages of a magazine. He flashed a cheeky smile and shook hands, saying, "Welcome Ji, myself, Vinay Talwar." His Nike T-shirt, emblazoned with "Let's do it!", stretched over his bulging pectorals

"You are looking for a student's room, Bhaiyaji?" Vinay asked.

"Yes, but I have a limited budget," Samar replied.

"Don't worry, Ji. We have all kinds of rooms—students' rooms, PG rooms, shared rooms—all types. The best rooms in Rajendra Nagar are on my list. You did the right thing coming now; availability will get limited in a week," Vinay explained with enthusiasm.

"I will assign Pinto to assist you. He'll show you some rooms, and then we can figure out the next steps," he added.

"Fine, then," Samar agreed.

He deputed Pinto, the loudly dressed fellow, to accompany Samar on a tour of the rental rooms.

Pinto started his scooter, and they set off.

Samar thought to himself, "This idiot will break my bones!" He dreaded another round of bumpy, scary rides. Pinto skillfully navigated through the narrow streets of Old Rajendra Nagar, with Samar on the back, but Samar hated riding pillion with him.

The rear entrance to the first property made a poor first impression. The room was tiny, barely bigger than a pigeonhole, with only a narrow vent for air. A world map adorned the wall, which desperately needed a fresh coat of paint. Pinto tried to promote it, saying, "Business is brisk at this time of the year. Rooms are limited, Bhaiya!"

At the second property, a skinny man wearing an over-worn VIP vest and crumpled pyjamas opened the gate. He looked annoyed and seemed to silently scold Samar, as if to say, "You're interrupting my studies! You don't look like you'll pass the IAS!"

"There's only one room available; the other two are taken," Pinto informed Samar.

The room appeared to be an architectural wonder. Once inside, it was impossible to tell whether it was night or day; it was completely light-proof!

Samar disapproved of the second property as well. Pinto then suggested two or three-bedroom floors. *"Mere pass floors bhi hain* on sharing basis! Price *thoda zyaada hoga, Bhaiya!"*

Next, he showed Samar a single-floor property on the second floor with two small rooms, a common living area, and a bathroom. A poster on the wall proclaimed, "We shall overcome!" and the smell of fresh paint filled the air.

When they returned to Talwar Properties, Vinay Talwar asked, "So, *Bhaiyaji, Kuch pasand aaya?"*

"Well, the property on the second floor looks good," Samar replied.

"It will cost eight thousand," Vinay said.

"Oh! That's too high for me," Samar responded.

"I can give you a discount of two thousand."

"Still too high."

"Six thousand is the best offer. Only for you, Bhaiyaji, since you came early."

"Okay. I will contact you once I find other flatmates," Samar said.

"Rooms are limited, so *jaldi decision le lo,* Bhaiya!" Pinto shouted as he dropped him off at the bus stop.

On the bus ride to Dwarka, Samar remained standing the entire trip, even though a few seats were empty. His bottom was sore from the bumpy scooter ride!

***

Three days later, Samar took another bus to Old Rajendra Nagar. He arrived around 11 am outside Rajan's IAS Study Circle to submit his admission form. Young aspirants from all over India swarmed the entire staircase to the first floor of the building and the area in front of the institute.

Everyone seems to be an IAS aspirant. How will the UPSC accommodate so many?

There was a long queue to submit the forms.

"Is this the queue for admission?" Samar asked.

"Of course! *Lag jao race main!*" a boy commented.

"*Hum bhi hain josh mein! Baatein kar hosh mein!*" mimicked another fellow, standing right behind the previous one. A peal of laughter broke out among the aspirants at his poor imitation of Shah Rukh Khan from *Josh*. Samar joined the queue.

The line was quite long, starting from the lane in front of the building and meandering its way up to Elangovan's tiny cubicle through the stairways, accompanied by murmurs and chatter. Aspirants had come alone or in the company of other aspirants. Some appeared to have arrived straight from the railway station, luggage in hand. The female aspirants were typically accompanied by a father, brother, or cousin.

The boy standing in front of Samar glanced back and said, "Hi, I am Udit… Udit Koppikar. Are you looking for admission?"

Before Samar could reply, the fellow behind him said coyly, "No, no… we are auditioning for the hero's role in a Juhi Chawla starrer!"

Udit chuckled, while Samar half-smiled.

"Of course, we are all standing in the queue to get admission to Rajan's—the No.1 IAS churning factory in India! By the way, I am Sunny Singh from Chandigarh." He leaned forward to shake their hands.

"Hi, I'm Samar Sarma from Guwahati. I came to Delhi a few days back."

"The way everyone is jostling for admission here, it seems like they have a guarantee scheme for an IAS seat!" Udit joked, eager to impress Sunny Singh.

"If I get admission to Rajan's today, I will feel like I have already cleared the exam!" Sunny snickered instead.

The trio continued their discussions. Udit, a Marathi boy from Mumbai, was an Arts graduate, while Sunny, a *Jatt* Punjabi, had graduated from Chandigarh. Finding accommodation in the vicinity was on their agenda. Samar mentioned the rentals he had visited through Talwar Properties. They agreed to go on a "Mission *Gharonda*" together afterwards.

They had to wait for another two hours before it was their turn. Elangovan quickly scanned Samar's form, assigned a serial number, and instructed him to deposit the requisite course fee of 25,500 rupees with the cashier in the adjacent room.

"Mr Samar, you are one of the late candidates. You cannot choose your session. We will assign you to any of the available sessions."

"How many sessions do you have, Sir?"

"A morning, an afternoon, and an evening session. Just look out for your name on the board later."

Oh no! I'm on the waitlist!

He cursed himself for being late that morning. He found Udit downstairs. Neither of them had the option to choose their session. Five minutes later, Sunny also joined them.

"So, are you both also on the waitlist?" Sunny asked.

"Yes," Udit replied feebly.

"Come on, let's have some food. Then, we can visit the property dealer Samar mentioned. What do you say?" Sunny suggested.

"Sounds good to me," Samar replied.

They grabbed a meal at a local *dhaba*. After they finished

eating, Sunny said, "Let's go for 'Mission *Gharonda*'!" They high-fived excitedly.

They stepped into the premises of Talwar Properties, where Vinay greeted them.

"Pinto will show you around. We can discuss afterwards," he said.

"Okay. Let's do it," Sunny responded.

Pinto drove the trio in a well-used Maruti Esteem, with loud Punjabi music blaring from the dashboard stereo, to a few rented accommodations. The group settled on the same accommodation on the second floor that Samar had liked during his last search. It had a separate side entrance, two bedrooms, a common living room, a bathroom, and a small kitchen. *"Ek Jabalpur waale Bhaiya aur ek Kanpur wale Bhaiya* cleared the IAS, *isiliye khaali huya tha pichle mahiney!"* Pinto announced, adding, "Lucky Flat!"

That extra bit of information sealed the deal for them!

Back at Talwar Properties' office, they negotiated a deal. The agreement involved an advance deposit equivalent to two months' rent and a security deposit of 10,000. Vinay Talwar took a commission of another four thousand.

"Now, we need to check our names on the list," Udit reminded them.

"Let's do it!" Sunny said enthusiastically.

The trio made their way to Rajan's notice board to check the list. They had been allotted evening sessions.

***

CHAPTER 2

Old Rajendra Nagar is the Mecca for IAS aspirants. Originally called Rajendra Nagar, named after the first President, it was a refugee colony established during the early years after Partition. The predominantly Punjabi community engaged in various businesses, improving their social standing. Numerous IAS coaching centres mushroomed over the last few decades, ensuring a steady flow of IAS aspirants to the roughly seven thousand rental rooms. Nearly every house in the 63 blocks offers rented or paying guest accommodation, floors, or hostels. Property dealers like Vinay Talwar became wealthy by arranging accommodation for inexperienced aspirants. Landlords often quoted above-market rents, and the naïve aspirants, having little alternative, accepted these offers after some negotiation. Many landlords relied solely on rental income. The success of such businesses led many property owners and dealers to acquire additional properties for rental purposes over the years. Dhabas and other eateries thrived on the influx of aspirants, offering a range of cuisines from Punjabi, Bengali, Marathi, and Gujarati to South Indian. Shops and PCOs operated photocopiers as a side business to meet the high demand for copies of books and notes. Landlords, property dealers, dhaba owners, shopkeepers, and aspirants co-existed in a symbiotic relationship of love and hate.

Samar was the first to shift to the rented accommodation within two days, being uncomfortable staying with relatives. Sunny and Udit moved in the next day.

Udit occupied the single room, while Samar and Sunny shared the larger one. Local service providers quickly delivered their cards for tiffin, retail food, ironing, and laundry services. "Free Home Delivery *Milega! Aap log sirf padhai karo!*" It was amusing how swiftly news of their move spread among local service providers. They ordered tiffin services for lunch and dinner according to their food preferences: Udit chose Marathi tiffin, Sunny opted for Punjabi, and Samar, finding no Assamese option, settled for 'less spicy' tiffin. They hired a maid to clean and mop on alternate days.

Gradually, they grew familiar with each other over breakfast at a nearby dhaba or during breaks after study sessions.

Samar, 24, was slim, about 5 feet 9 inches tall, clean-shaven, wheatish-skinned, and quite handsome. He was shy, subtle, pleasant, and friendly by nature. Udit Koppikar, short-statured and dark-skinned, was pensive and moody. Both his parents were IAS officers in the Maharashtra cadre. He was confident he would clear the exam, as his parents had succeeded before. Sunny Singh, 23, was tall. His good looks, sharp features, and toned physique complemented his cheerful, witty personality, full of self-confidence. An athlete, he loved most sports, especially football. His father was a neurosurgeon, and his mother was a homemaker. His family included many doctors and engineers, but no civil servants, and it was expected that he would become one.

Gradually, they settled in, eagerly waiting for the classes to commence. They discussed newspapers, reference books, popular options that fetched high marks, issues like splitting rent and electricity bills, and more. Studies had not begun in earnest yet, as they were waiting for classes to begin. In the evening, they explored the area to relax. Sunny had a roving eye, and would ogle at the girls passing by. Udit lectured him to focus on his goal, and not to distract them.

***

The first-day session was to start at 5.30 pm. There was palpable excitement mixed with some nervous anticipation. Samar, Sunny, and Udit ate their tiffin lunch together, took a quick nap, and then got ready for their first day at Rajan's IAS Study Circle. They dressed in crisp, freshly ironed shirts and trousers, looking like young marketing executives. They headed to the tea stall across the road in front of the coaching centre for tea and snacks. Other aspirants arrived on foot, by bike, or in cars.

The lecture hall had 12 rows of chairs, with eight on each side of a central aisle. Only a few seats were vacant. The aspirants were in their early twenties, from affluent, middle-class, or less privileged backgrounds. About 30 per cent of them were females.

A boy from Chandigarh, who knew Sunny, waved at him. Sunny sat next to him in the third row. A new friend from Mumbai called out Udit's name. Udit settled down next to him in the fifth row. Samar did not know anyone except his flatmates. He found an aisle seat in the third-last row. The chairs were uncomfortable, with mesh seats made of plastic strings on a wooden frame. A wooden plank attached to one side of the armrest served as a writing desk.

"Only three or four from this class might succeed. I need to be one of them!" Samar silently promised himself.

At exactly 5.30 pm, a tall gentleman in formal attire and a tie entered the room, escorted by Elangovan, and headed to the podium. He adjusted the microphone to address the aspirants.

"Dear aspirants, your presence here today sets you apart from others. You are future civil servants, and I feel privileged to address you. I am Mr Ravi, and I will guide you over the next few months on your exciting journey toward success."

Mr Ravi's opening remarks captured everyone's attention.

"You have gathered here to become a civil servant and serve your country. I am glad, and I assume each of you has decided to bring about meaningful change in society and contribute to your country's development and growth."

"Do you agree? Anyone who disagrees with me? Anyone!"

He paused, scanning the entire hall.

"As if someone will get up and say 'No'!" someone murmured, but it did not reach Mr Ravi's ears.

"The bureaucracy is the foundation of governance. It is the core machinery that frames laws, rules, policies, and guidelines, implements schemes, and enforces laws. It is the face of the government to the public. Bureaucrats operate the Election Commission, the District Magistrate's office, the Revenue and Income Tax departments, Railways, the CAG, and the Ministry of External Affairs. They are indispensable, regardless of what others may say. Therefore, I am here to guide you to become one, so you can serve our country and find satisfaction in life."

The speech gave Samar goosebumps.

The monologue continued…

"But I need one promise from each of you. Each one of you has to promise today, right here, right now, that you will dedicate and devote the next few months to preparing for this exam and nothing else. No distractions... absolutely no distractions! Only commitment. Make this promise to yourself, and I assure you, you will carve your way to success. I am not saying it will be easy; it is hard. You will feel frustrated, low, and like quitting, but if you persevere and sail through the hard times, you will finally make it. However, not all of you will succeed. Compete amongst yourselves. You are not here to make friends or to find a girlfriend or boyfriend," he added as some aspirants chuckled loudly. "You are competitors. So treat one another as competitors and try to outdo each other in this race."

Just then, the two halves of the main entry door to the class were flung open with more force than necessary, banging against the wall. Everyone's eyes turned to see a pretty girl, dressed in a light pink *chikan salwar*, rush into the class, clutching her sling bag alongside, her *dupatta* sweeping the floor behind her. She quickly spotted an empty chair at the back and hurried towards it, avoiding prying eyes. The empty chair was second to an occupied one on the aisle where Samar was seated. She looked at Samar, hinting at him to move to the empty chair. Samar shifted to the vacant seat while the girl settled into the chair vacated by Samar. Mr Ravi looked slightly disturbed by the untoward interruption.

"I need one more promise from all of you. Just be in class before time. You can't aspire to be a good civil servant if you do not respect time."

The girl felt like ducking herself under the seat, knowing well that the remark was directed at her. The class went quiet.

Mr Ravi paused, looking at the girl, and said, "Young lady, please do not take it personally. This advice was for everyone here."

Mr Ravi resumed his speech, trying to instil discipline and dedication among the aspirants. The opening lecture was effective. The air was thick with hope, promise, aspiration, excitement, and determination. Like a motivational guru, he energized the aspirants, and most of them seemed to have entered a trance.

They announced a fifteen-minute break. The class was to reconvene at 6.45 pm. Most aspirants trickled out for a tea or coffee break. Some were looking around to connect with others.

I have struggled a lot! The tuition classes, Maloti bow's mocking remarks…

Samar was lost in thought, reflecting on the discourse. He felt a tap on his shoulder. The girl sitting next to him flashed a bright smile and said, "It looks like you have made yourself a promise!"

"Yes, I promised not to be late to classes," Samar chuckled feebly.

"Very funny. Already, I have managed to give enough *masala* today." The girl made a face.

"By the way, I am Abha Deswal from Sonepat."

She flashed another smile. Samar managed a faint smile and said, "Hello Abha ji, I am Samar Sarma from Guwahati."

"Oh, I see! It must be an amazing place!"

Her tied hair fell loose as she tossed her head. She tied them back and looked at Samar. Her direct gaze made him shy and jittery.

"You have been to Guwahati? It is Assam's capital," he blurted out nervously, unable to think of anything else.

"No... I have not been there. This is the first time I have come out of my home to Delhi." She continued to look at him.

"By the way, I know Guwahati is the capital of Assam. Otherwise, if I didn't even know that, I shouldn't be trying for this exam!" She chuckled enough to embarrass Samar.

"So, where are you staying?"

"I have rented a flat with two other boys near the water tank road."

"Oh … Okay. I am in a hotel. It's costing me a lot. I am looking for rented accommodation or a PG nearby. Can you help me find one?"

Samar was about to respond when she repeated, "Can you help?"

"Well, maybe I can. I know a property dealer, Abha*ji*."

"That's wonderful. Actually, I got to class late, walking all the way from my hotel in Karol Bagh. By the way, call me Abha. Abha*ji* feels like *behenji*. Do you think I look like a *behenji*?" She grimaced and pretended to look upset.

"No … No… I didn't mean that! You are…"

"You are what? Pretty? I know that!" she smiled.

"Yes. Sure," he managed shyly.

They had to stop their conversation, as Mr Ravi returned to resume the class. He suggested a list of books to refer to and read.

"Read newspapers early in the day, every day! *The Hindu, The Economic Times*. Read the notes the same day after class, invariably, and revise again so that it gets registered in the mind."

Further, Mr Ravi informed that he would teach Polity, Science & Technology, and Current Affairs. He took the names of other lecturers: Indian Economy by Mr Kathuria, Geography by Mr Manocha, Ancient History by…. Medieval History by…

The introductory class finally finished. Most of the aspirants were quite impressed.

"Can we look for the rentals right away?" Abha was waiting in the corridor as Samar came out of the class.

"Not now. I will speak to the property dealer and fix up a time as soon as possible."

"Sounds good."

Samar did not know what to say and stood blankly.

"You don't speak much, do you?" Abha chuckled.

Samar's face turned red.

"Okay. I won't bother you much. It's getting dark, so I need to return to my hotel. See you in class!"

Abha walked briskly towards Karol Bagh as Samar watched her walk away.

"Who was that pretty girl?" Sunny caught up with Samar and patted him on the shoulder.

"Oh... Abha… a friend."

"Oh, a friend… You know her?"

"No … No, just met her in the class."

"Why is she walking away so fast?"

"She is staying in a hotel in Karol Bagh. It is getting dark, so…"

"Why didn't you walk her to the hotel? Where is chivalry these days?" Sunny interrupted, lightly punching Samar in the chest.

"What more did she say?"

"She was looking for a rented room."

"You offered your room?" Sunny chuckled.

Samar made a face. Then he said, "You seemed really interested in her. Why don't you offer yours instead?"

"I would have if she had approached me. Such a pretty girl. But now, I will not become a *haddi* between you two lovers!" Sunny laughed.

By then, Udit caught up with them.

"Mr Ravi made the same speech last year," Udit said to impress them.

"How do you know?" Sunny asked.

"I have heard his introductory class."

"Really! Do people record such classes? That is funny!"

"Yes, they do? I have all his lectures. A veteran aspirant shipped all his lectures on a few pen drives to me in Mumbai."

"That's hilarious!" Sunny said.

"What is so hilarious about it? Serious candidates do such things, Sunny."

"Oh… Okay. I get the point."

***

The next day, Samar found Abha waiting for him outside the centre's entrance. She suggested having coffee together.

"Don't worry. The treat is on me!"

They ordered coffee at a cafe across the road.

Abha tied her long hair just below the nape, letting it fall freely down her back. The silky, freshly shampooed hair flowed sideways as the fan's breeze brushed through. She was very fair, so fair that the greenish tinge of her veins was faintly visible on her neck and the sides of her cheeks. Her hazel eyes complemented her light, supple skin. She was tall for a girl, nearly as tall as Samar. She had a wholesome figure—broad shoulders, a shapely bosom, and a narrow waist.

The lemon-yellow salwar and dark-green churidaar look stunning. No, she is stunning!

Why am I looking at her again and again? What will she think?

A strange sensation ran through Samar, sitting across from Abha. He had rarely encountered such a confident, upfront girl before. The few girls he knew back home were shy. Her confidence made quite an impression on Samar. He cursed himself.

After the coffee, they sat side by side in class. Samar ignored Sunny's mischievous winks.

Later, Samar and Abha visited the Talwar Properties premises. Abha seemed to have a way with men. Vinay Talwar, too, was charmed by her.

His teeth might fall out with that puppy grin! Moron! Men! Delhi Men!

"Pinto! Get some cold drinks!" shouted Vinay.

He offered to take them around in his swanky car to show a few rentals.

"Madam Ji, the car is a bit unclean at the back. Please sit in the front."

So, Abha sat in the front seat. He drove around to show a few options. Strangely, Vinay offered discounted rates for the same premises, which he had quoted at a higher price to Samar and his flatmates.

Men! Delhi Men!

Abha chose a single room with an attached bathroom in a girls-only hostel. It was a few blocks away from Samar's floor. Abha got the room at 10 per cent below the listed price—"special discount only for you, Abha Ji."

"Thank you so much, Vinay Ji. I appreciate that," Abha smiled back.

"Mention not, Abha Ji. *Aap ke jaise customers thodi na roz roz aate hain!*" Vinay looked foolish, at least to Samar, as he grinned widely.

Vinay brandished his card. "You can call for any help."

"That's good. Thank you."

Vinay offered to drop her off at the hotel.

Abha shifted into the rented room the next morning. Vinay sent his helper to assist with the move.

The following day, Abha greeted Samar before class.

"Hey Samar, how are you?" she asked.

Samar smiled faintly.

"Why do you speak so little, Samar?"

"Because wise men speak less and act more."

"Ha Ha Ha! You do have a sense of humour, though." Abha gazed into his eyes.

"Probably, better than Vinay Talwar."

"Aaawww! Someone's jealous!"

"No… No… I mean… I am just saying…" Samar turned red instantly, looking away to avoid her teasing eyes.

"Anyway, I won't tease you further. Listen, I am going to Sonepat for three days to pick up some stuff. Make sure you take good notes. I will need them!"

"Sure, Abha."

How can I say no!

***

CHAPTER 3

A week of classes had passed. The routine settled for the trio. They bought reference books and NCERT books for standards IX-XII, recommended by other experienced aspirants. The trio spent considerable time on newspapers, mainly *The Hindu,* like a hawk hunting prey, scribbling notes, and pasting important newspaper cuttings. They regularly discussed key issues to shape their views. They diligently revised their class notes. Occasionally, to escape boredom from the tiffin food, they skipped it and went to a dhaba in Old Rajendra Nagar. The Popular Dhaba was quite popular, being affordable for aspirants from the nearby coaching centres.

Abha returned from Sonepat in a week, bringing extra luggage filled with clothes and essentials. Her brother, Rohit, dropped her off. On the day of her return, she came to Samar's floor.

She knocked on the door on the staircase. It was closed from the inside. Sunny was at the door.

"Hi Sunny! How are you?" Abha smiled.

"Hi! I am fine. How about you? You were not coming to classes?" Sunny asked.

"Oh yes... I went to my hometown to pick up some stuff. Did I miss any important topics?"

"Yes, I think so. Anyway, come inside."

She followed him down the long, three-sided, narrow passage that also served as a balcony into the living room. The room was basic, with just a table and four plastic chairs provided by the landlord. No curtains.

"Let me guess, you were looking for me or Udit, not Samar, right?"

They both laughed.

"Samar, I have a surprise for you. Come out," Sunny called.

Samar was surprised to see Abha in the living room.

"Hi! You are back?"

"Yes. I am back."

"You both carry on. I need to do something," Sunny interrupted. He winked at Samar and went inside.

The brief silence was awkward. Samar did not expect her to visit him unannounced.

"Oh! First, have a seat, Abha." Samar pulled up a chair for her.

"I am feeling jittery! I missed quite a lot of classes," Abha said, sitting down.

"You did!"

"What all did I miss?"

"Mr Ravi finished the Fundamental Rights and Directive Principles of State Policies," he replied.

"What to do? Mom and cousin sisters insisted I should stay back till the weekend," Abha said, making a face.

"Don't worry. I am sure you will catch up."

"I came to collect your notes."

"Oh! I am revising them till evening."

"Then, do me a favour. Can you get them photocopied, and give them to me in the evening class?" She requested.

Samar nodded.

"Great. Thank you so much."

She got up to leave. At the stairs, she said in a low voice, "Do you want to grab lunch with me at the dhaba? I am starving, and would love to have a nice companion."

Stay away from her! She is a distraction!

Samar made a weak excuse. "I was in the middle of studies."

"C'mon Samar! It's OK to relax a bit. Heavens will not fall if you don't study for two hours," she insisted.

Go! It would be a welcome change from the tiffin food. Eating out once in a while could be managed without hurting your limited budget.

Samar quickly changed into a fresh T-shirt and jeans while she waited downstairs.

The Popular Dhaba was a ten-minute walk from his house. It was usually full. After a ten-minute wait, they got a table. A waiter hastily placed a plate of onion and cucumber slices, along with mixed pickles, before them.

"What is there on the menu?" Abha asked him.

The waiter recited the menu in a single breath: *Dal Tadka*, *Makhani*, *Paneer* Butter *Masala*, Chicken Fry, Butter Chicken,

Naan, tandoori rotis…

Abha ordered a bottle of mineral water, a plate of Butter Chicken, a yellow *Dal Tadka,* and *tandoori rotis.*

"The aroma of *ghee* and food is making me extremely hungry," Abha said.

"Me too!" said Samar.

Their food arrived in 10 minutes. It was delicious.

It's good that she made me come out.

His mind and heart conflicted.

Did you come to Delhi for romance?

Stop bothering me. Let me enjoy the moment.

Have you forgotten what Ravi Sir said about distractions?

No, I haven't. Just let me relax now.

She looks bubbly and cute when she talks.

Abha had completed English Honours from Sonepat. She had to struggle to continue her studies in the male-dominated, feudal-minded household. Her father and elder brother had planned to marry her off after graduation, but she put up a spirited resistance and came to Delhi to prepare for the UPSC civil services exams.

"I want to break free and lead a life where I can make an independent decision without struggling or rebelling," she said. "They have given me one year to crack the exam. If I fail, I will have to get married."

Samar listened to her intently, fascinated by her spirited personality. It was difficult to guess that behind that charming facade, she had hidden her pain and struggle. Samar felt overwhelmed with sympathy for her.

"I want to tour the world and settle down in a big city like Delhi. Now tell me about yourself. I know very little about you!" she said.

He briefly told her about his family background, his strained relationship with his sister-in-law, and his struggles.

"So, we both are strugglers in one way or the other," Abha said. Then she added teasingly, "Enough of serious stuff. Tell me, do you have a girlfriend?"

"I don't have one. I liked a girl in my neighbourhood back home, but I was too shy to approach her." Samar blushed.

"Gosh! You blush like a girl!"

Samar blushed a deeper red.

"Let's head to the photocopy shop," Abha suggested after they had finished their meal.

At the photocopy shop, they got copies made of the notes and then walked back to Abha's place.

On his way back, Samar pondered over Abha's struggles and her determination to resist her family's feudal mindset, and carve out a life for herself. He was deeply impressed by her outspoken nature, confidence, fighting spirit, and willpower.

Abha is beautiful, both inside and out. She is a fighter!

I wish I could support her, and help her fulfil her dreams and goals.

***

Two weeks had passed since Samar and Abha went out for lunch. A special bond had formed between them. They started doing things together, like drinking tea at the tea stall before the classes, sitting together in the classes, and visiting the general stores.

On one such occasion, after buying some things, they walked home together and reached the street adjacent to Abha's hostel.

"See you tomorrow. Study hard," Samar said, extending his right hand for a handshake as usual.

Abha's hand lingered in his. Then she said, "Wait a moment! I want to hug you."

Samar smiled incredulously as Abha hugged him tightly. It was the first time they had close contact. Samar hugged her back.

"I can feel the loud thumping of your heart," Abha said softly.

He wished the moment would last forever.

Abha drew back and gave him a peck on his cheek, smiling.

"Now, study well!" she chuckled.

He felt a powerful urge to pull her and kiss her back, but he controlled himself.

"I will. That was a booster dose," Samar said softly.

"Aahhaa! Someone has learned the art of flirting!"

Samar blushed.

"Good night. See you tomorrow," Abha shouted as she rushed up the stairs of her hostel.

Does she feel for me like I do? I think she does; otherwise, why would she hug and kiss me? Why would she spend so much time with me? She is beautiful and unique. She can have anyone, but she chose me!

***

A month had passed. Classes for Geography, History, and Economics commenced. The classes were interesting and interactive. The aspirants became consistent and serious. A wide range of topics was covered—the 16 Mahajanapadas; the rise of Magadha; the Mauryas; Ashoka's empire; Buddhism and Jainism; the Chola, Pandya, and Chera dynasties; Kanishka; Harsh Vardhan; the Tughlaq, Lodhi, and Mughal dynasties; the climatic zones, rivers, sanctuaries, and national parks of India; economic concepts like trade deficit, fiscal policy, taxation policy, and investment policy.

Meanwhile, the bond between Samar and Abha deepened. They became inseparable, spending three or four hours together every evening, before and after classes. As the weeks passed, Samar grew increasingly infatuated with Abha.

One evening, on returning after walking Abha to her hostel, Samar found Udit and Sunny relaxing on the balcony.

Udit was in a pensive mood, while Sunny was jovial.

"Our lover boy is back after dropping off Abha *bhabhi*!" Sunny grinned and pumped his fists in the air.

"*Arrey*, there is nothing like that! We are just friends. She is alone here, so I help her out," Samar mumbled and blushed. "Yes, we can see that. Our Prince Charming!" Sunny patted his back and chuckled.

"It's none of my business, Samar, but I think you are getting distracted!" Udit said seriously.

"Why do you say that?" Sunny asked.

"Because he is forgetting why he came to Delhi. This is the time to devote our time and energy to the UPSC and nothing else!"

"Come on, Udit, let the *bacha* have some fun. We can't study like robots all the time," Sunny said.

"It is just a bit of friendly advice. The rest is up to Samar."

"You are right, Udit," Samar said thoughtfully.

"Don't mind me saying so, but try to control your schoolboy crush before it's too late."

Udit's terse words pinched Samar sharply. Irritated with himself for loitering around with Abha, he ate dinner, went straight to his room, and studied till late in the night.

The next day, Samar woke up earlier than usual and started revising his notes. However, thoughts about Abha distracted him.

What is happening to me? Why am I getting drawn to her? Did I come all the way to Delhi for this? I must concentrate on my preparation. I have already wasted many precious hours with her. I must keep my distance from her now.

That evening, when Abha arrived to walk with him to Rajan's, he excused himself, saying, "Abha, you go on. Something has come up. I will join you later in the class."

"Oh! But what about our coffee?"

"I won't be able to join you today. Sorry."

"Okay. See you in class."

Abha left, confused.

Samar walked to the class with Sunny, and did not sit next to Abha.

The next evening, when Abha arrived, Samar made up another excuse. "I have a mild stomach pain. I think coffee does not suit me."

"Okay. I will see you in class."

"Sure."

Samar kept himself busy with Sunny and his friends in the class, ignoring Abha completely. His odd behaviour puzzled Abha.

For the next couple of days, he devoted additional time to studies and interacted more closely with his roommates, especially Sunny. He arrived just in time for classes and interacted with other classmates to avoid Abha.

Abha understood that Samar was trying to avoid her, but it didn't bother her.

How long will this awkward, gawky fellow ignore me? He will come running to me some day... till then, let it be so!

She ignored him, too, and looked for an opportunity to make new friends.

***

CHAPTER 4

It was the last week of October when Elangovan announced a test on Polity. There were loud murmurs in the class.

It had been a while since Abha had spoken to Samar, except for a distant 'Hi' or 'Hello'. The Polity test made her slightly nervous, and she wanted to talk to someone.

She approached Samar after the class. "Hey Samar, how have you been? How are your studies going?"

"I am fine. My studies are not too good, not too bad," he replied disinterestedly.

"I find it tough to follow Polity. It is so dry! I was wondering if we could study together for the test?" she asked hopefully.

"I think it would be better to study individually. In case you have any doubts, I can try to clarify them a day or two before the test," Samar mumbled, avoiding her eyes.

"Fine, then. Best of Luck!" Abha retorted and walked off.

Samar was relieved that she had not insisted. Her proximity made him jittery and nervous.

There was an unspoken competition among Samar, Udit, and Sunny. The trio studied hard for the approaching test.

Udit joined a group composed solely of Marathi aspirants. By now, he had developed a poor opinion of his flatmates. "It's better to prepare in my core group. My roommates are not too serious. One flirts with every girl on the street, and the other one is Abha's *pappu*!" he thought.

Sunny had formed a cosmopolitan group with a few boys and girls who attended classes at Rajan's.

Samar did not have a positive view of group study and refused to join any group, even though Sunny asked him to join his group. Samar had completed his graduation in Political Science from Cotton College, and considered Polity to be his forte.

Finally, the D-day arrived!

The Polity paper consisted of short, medium, and long questions to be answered in 60 minutes. The atmosphere in the classroom was serious, as if the students were appearing for a real General Studies paper.

Samar found the questions challenging. They were analytical and opinion-based, whereas he had been studying mere facts.

After two days, Mr Ravi discussed the test. He called out the names of students and announced their marks. Aspirants scored from as low as 15 marks to as high as 89. Udit scored 67 out of a hundred, Sunny scored 79, Abha scored 36, and Samar, forty-two.

After announcing the results, Mr Ravi said, "Now, those of you who scored above 75, raise your hands."

About 30 people raised their hands.

"You all have done well. Carry on with the excellent work."

"Those of you who scored between 50-75 need to improve," he continued. "And those of you who scored below 50 need to put in a lot of effort. Please raise your hands. You are already running behind in the race!"

Samar, Abha, and 30 other students hesitantly raised their hands, embarrassed, and dejected amid the aspirants with higher scores.

Mr Ravi discussed each question and its suitable answer. He quoted lines from selected answers amongst the aspirants, like Sunny.

"It is not only important to revise the notes but also to analyze and brainstorm," said Mr Ravi. He suggested the students should form small study groups and discuss the subjects or topics.

Samar walked back home dejectedly. Udit's mocking smile when Samar's marks were announced flashed repeatedly before his eyes. He was extremely embarrassed and disappointed.

Abha, who was walking about 50 feet ahead of Samar, saw him coming and decided to wait for him. As he was about to pass her she called out to him, "Samar, can I talk to you for a second?"

He started at the sound of her voice and averted his gaze.

"I told you we should have studied and discussed together," Abha said. "Most people who scored well had done group study. Look at Sunny and Udit. Ankita and Neha were part of Sunny's group, and they both did well. Otherwise, what does Ankita know about Polity? I only see her flirting around with boys."

"Hmm."

"I don't know what's wrong with you. You were so friendly with me, but now, you just keep avoiding me," Abha remarked.

"Nothing like that," Samar mumbled.

"I know it. I don't need any explanation. It's your choice," She continued, "But did you notice how Udit and Ankita were acting? They behaved as if they have already cleared the IAS!"

She felt embarrassed to have scored so low, far lower than some other 'undeserving' girls. Scores of other aspirants had fared far better than expected.

"Abha, I am already very upset," Samar muttered.

"So am I! If my brother comes to know that I am not doing well here, he will come, pack me off to Sonepat, and marry me off!" Abha said loudly.

"All right. What's your point?"

"My point is we should try to study together," Abha said.

"Okay."

Samar and Abha started walking.

"We will study on our own, and discuss together now and then. Is it a deal?"

"Done!" said Samar.

They walked together silently for a while, more relaxed now.

"Can we go out for dinner now?" Abha asked.

He nodded.

"It's nice to see your smile again!" Abha patted him on the back.

Samar wanted to avoid his roommates on that disastrous day. Abha, a fellow sufferer, seemed to be the better option. They walked to Popular Dhaba, and ordered an oil-laden Punjabi meal.

Abha held onto his arm as they walked back home. They reached her hostel. At that late hour, the street was desolate and dark, but it was a full moon night. They gazed at one another, and Abha planted a kiss on his cheek. Samar grabbed her by the arm and awkwardly pulled her close to him.

"*Oye hoye! Oye hoye! Kya scene hain!*"

A group of local teenage boys passing by on a motorbike whistled and cheered. "Carry on, champ!"

They pulled away abruptly. Abha laughed nervously, and Samar blushed. Abha kissed him on the lips fleetingly and rushed upstairs. Samar stood there, flabbergasted.

On his way back home, Samar felt conflicting emotions. As he entered, Sunny remarked, "What's up, dude? I saw you with Abha. All back to normal?"

Samar was in no mood for light banter. Without replying, he settled down on his bed and closed his eyes.

The long, silky flowing hair... the dangling black metal earrings... her svelte figure... everything about Abha was lovely... she had verve!

His heart trumped the rational voice of the mind and overflowed with emotions. However, he was unsure whether Abha would reciprocate his feelings. Still, he decided that they would fight their battles together.

***

The next morning, Samar woke up in a cheerful mood. He read the newspapers, noted down a few important facts, and pasted newspaper cuttings in his scrapbook. He was glad to see Moorty's *idlis* and chutney hanging in a small polythene bag on the doorknob. Moorty had a brisk side business supplying breakfast prepared by his wife to students. Then, Samar sat down to revise the previous day's notes.

About an hour later, his thoughts drifted to what Abha might be doing at the moment.

Is she studying? Is she thinking about me?

Samar was keen to create a close, cohesive group. His flatmates might have fared better because of group studies. It allowed them to interact, discuss, and exchange ideas. It also saved time.

Around 11 am, he strolled to Abha's hostel. Abha stayed on the first floor, and her window was open sideways. She peeped out at his call and flashed a bright smile. Moments later, she was downstairs.

"Good Morning, Sunshine! How did you forget the way so early?" she teased.

"Stop teasing me. I think you were right. Let's form a selective group to study."

"That's excellent," Abha jumped at the idea.

"But it should be a small group."

"Okay. I will ask one or two of my acquaintances. But where will we assemble?"

"At my place. And we are the first two official members!" Samar said excitedly, extending his hand to shake hers.

"That's great."

The group study commenced over the weekend. Two girls from Abha's hostel and one boy from the class, Vipul, joined the group. The group study took place either at Samar's place or at Vipul's, twice or thrice a week. The discussions appeared to be fruitful and satisfactory.

Besides the group study, Samar and Abha met almost every day. Both had Public Administration as their first option. They mostly met during the day to discuss the concepts of Pub-Ad, as it was popularly called on his floor. They resumed their coffee sessions in the evening, before class, and occasionally shared lunch or dinner. Once in a while, they went to the movies together. People who knew them regarded Samar and Abha as a couple. Samar and Abha avoided acknowledging it, saying, "We are studying together. We are just good friends."

***

Two more months passed. Geography and Ancient and Medieval History classes ended. Statistics and Science & Technology classes began. By then, the aspirants had developed a fair idea of UPSC preparations.

Samar enjoyed the major topics of the Indian Economy. Mr Kathuria's clear approach made concepts like Inflation, Monetary Policy in India, Banks, and Financial markets relatable. Samar devoted more time to those topics compared to the dull ones of Indian Agriculture, Poverty, Inequality, and Unemployment.

A test on the Indian Economy was announced in the third week of November.

The next day, the results were announced in class. Udit scored 53. Sunny and Samar scored well, securing 82 and 76, respectively, while Abha scored 62. Udit was sullen and withdrawn for a few days.

***

UPSC published the notification for the Civil Services (Preliminary) Examination in the first week of December 2000. Popularly known as Prelims, it was scheduled for Sunday, May 19, 2001. The application forms were available at various places, including post offices. The Rajendra Nagar Post Office was crowded with long queues of aspirants or their relatives, jostling for the forms.

Samar joined the queue to pay the requisite fees. An elderly gentleman asked him, "Which form are you collecting, Beta?"

"The Civil Services Examination form," Samar replied with a faint smile.

"That is a prestigious exam!" said the man. "I am a retired section officer from the central government. I'm sure you will crack it. May God bless you."

The elderly gentleman's words warmed Samar's heart.

I will be an IAS officer in the top rung in the government sector someday! Yes, indeed!

Funny, superstitious practices were prevalent among aspirants for filling forms. Sceptical aspirants, too, turned religious overnight. They prayed vigorously and distributed *prasad* to street children. Mothers performed elaborate *pujas* to please the gods and evoke their blessings.

Most aspirants posted their forms to UPSC, while some deposited them at the facilitation counter at Dholpur House. Many aspirants, including Samar and Sunny, deposited their forms on the first day of submission to be allotted an examination centre at the UPSC premises.

***

The chilly winds from North India brought winter to Delhi in December, making studying in the dark, dingy rooms uncomfortable. Landlords provided heaters or blowers at additional charges.

The year 2001 commenced. The first two months passed quickly. Almost all subjects had been covered. Current Affairs was the last subject left for February. Students now spent more time studying at home, reaching classes just in time and reducing tea/coffee sessions.

Classes finally ended on March 5. Mr Ravi addressed the concluding session. Conveying his best wishes to everyone for the upcoming exam, he stressed self-discipline, dedication, hard work, and perseverance. His words were inspiring and reverberated in the minds of the students.

Samar and Abha studied together during the last three months as well. Samar was deeply in love with Abha by now and became more expressive of his feelings for her through holding hands, fleeting glances, parting embraces, and warm kisses. Abha, too, did not resist his moves. She dressed with care to please him—bright floral or pastel coloured salwars and long skirts were his favourites. She enjoyed his company, care, and attention, as well as her control over him, even though she was confused about the intensity of her own feelings. Yet, she gave the impression that she reciprocated his feelings. The situation suited her in a tough place like Delhi.

The aspirants were like migratory birds, leaving for their native places once the season was over. Some students moved to other places within Delhi, while many stayed back in Rajendra Nagar.

Udit left the flat to share a room with other Marathi friends, and Vipul, who was on good terms with Samar and Sunny, shifted in.

Meanwhile, Abha's father wanted her to return to Sonepat and prepare for the exam from there. She had no option but to agree. Samar was heartbroken, while Abha was dejected. Her relationship with Samar made her feel special.

Rohit, Abha's younger brother, was to pick her up late in the afternoon on March 12. Abha and Samar decided to spend the day together. Samar was in a sombre mood and hardly ate anything during lunch at the dhaba.

Abha saw genuine love, desolation, and desperation in his eyes.

He loves me. He cares for me. How I wish I could stay here! I hate my nagging family… their family honour… their izzat!

They walked quietly to her hostel after lunch. Samar became increasingly restive along the way.

"Why didn't you convince them to let you stay back in Delhi? You would have been in sync with the competitive environment here," protested Samar. "They will not let me write the exam if I resist. You don't know my father and brother!" Abha said despondently."I don't understand why they are so adamant about taking you back to Sonepat," Samar said in frustration.

"I don't know what else to do. I am abiding by their decision so that I can return to Delhi in the future," said Abha, trying to convince him.

Samar caught hold of her arms, turned her to face him, and asked, "What about us?"

"We will be together. I will return for sure, Samar. Now, don't make it harder for me," Abha replied softly, gazing into his eyes. "But I love you! Don't you know I love you?" Samar blurted out, tightening his grip on her arms. "Answer me! What about us? Don't you love me?"

"Samar, you are hurting me!" Abha protested.

"I love you… I love you a lot, Abha!" pleaded Samar.

Abha tried to free herself, but his grip was strong."I have loved you so much all these months, and you know, don't you?" said Samar, as he fought back his tears. "I know you love me, too. Otherwise, you wouldn't be with me. Tell me, Abha, before you leave today."

"Samar, let's not make it hard on ourselves. I like you… I enjoy your company. You are a nice person, but I don't fall in love so easily."

"But I love you. Why can't you love me back? You are lying… I know you are lying because you are scared of your family," Samar said agitatedly. "Don't worry about your family. I will convince them. Let us clear the UPSC and become financially independent."

"You are thinking too far, Samar. We don't know what is in store for us in the future."

Samar looked down at the ground, feeling helpless.

Abha lifted his chin, looked into his eyes, and said, "I like you a lot, but I have no choice right now. I expect you to understand my situation." She paused and added in a softer tone, "Right now, clearing the civil services exam should be your priority."

Her words jerked him back to reality. He released her arms. Tears trickled down his face, and Abha wiped them away.

"Samar, I want you to prepare well during these months and crack the Prelims. I will also study hard." She hugged him. "Don't worry. I will be back."

They walked in silence until they reached her hostel. After she went inside, he walked back slowly to his room with a heavy heart, helpless, restless, and dejected, but hopeful about seeing her again.

Abha left for Sonepat with her books and belongings. Her heart, too, was heavy, and she felt claustrophobic, on her way back to a restrictive, controlled life.

***

CHAPTER 5

The D-Day, May 19, 2001, arrived.

Samar's exam centre was at a government school in Gole Market. He had pre-booked an auto to avoid any problems on the day of the exam and arrived early at the centre. It was quite an active morning, buzzing with exam-related activities, for an otherwise laid-back Sunday in the area. A large board outside the centre's main gate displayed the room numbers assigned to the roll numbers. Aspirants arrived well before time and checked their allotted room numbers. Some were rushing through their notes in the small park next to the school, while others were chatting among themselves. Samar's room number was 8, his lucky number!.

Samar looked relaxed and calm. He had slept early the night before. His mind was reciting silent prayers. In the last two months, he had confined himself to his flat, studying and revising the class notes. He referred to his scrapbooks of newspaper cuttings, current affairs journals, *Economic Survey, Yojana, India Yearbook,* etc. The group study had stopped after Abha left.

He had no means to contact her since neither of them had a mobile phone. Abha had not given him her landline number. But her absence was beneficial as he could concentrate on his studies without much distraction. They had common Preliminary optionals, such as Pub-Ad. He had submitted their forms together, hoping to have the same centre.

His efforts bore fruit. About half an hour later, Abha arrived in a black Safari, escorted by her brother, Rohit. Rohit looked a quintessential *Jaat* fellow—light-skinned, tall, gym-toned physique. Samar and Abha noticed each other but avoided any exchange in Rohit's presence.

Entry was allowed in half an hour. Frisking began at the entry point. Only admit cards, pens, and pencils were allowed. *Calculators, bags, mobile phones, and lunch boxes not allowed* was written in bold letters at the entry gate.

Samar's room was on the ground floor of the right wing of the building. Once the students were seated, the invigilators went around the room with a sheet for students to sign against their roll number.

The loud ring of a bell at 10.30 am signalled the start of the exam.

"You can open the question booklet now and use the OMR answer sheet," announced an invigilator. "Public Administration" was inscribed at the top of the question booklet. The OMR sheet had instructions on how to fill it out. A section had questions with options a, b, c, and d to be encircled. Samar read the instructions twice and rechecked the filled-in details, such as roll numbers. He offered a silent prayer before opening the booklet. The optional paper had 120 questions.

The optional paper had 120 questions, the majority of which were average in terms of the level of difficulty for Samar. In some cases, the options were very close, leading to confusion. There was a pin-drop silence in the room as the students concentrated on their booklets.

Samar finished his paper well before time. In the last 25 minutes, he revised his answers and rechecked his entries in the OMR sheet. The last bell rang, and one invigilator collected the OMR sheets. The candidates were then instructed to leave the examination hall.

So far, so good.

There was a two-hour break before the next session. The students trickled out of the school premises. Many had their families or relatives waiting for them. Most people made a beeline for the mobile food carts in the lane, and local hawkers, too, did brisk business. Abha's Safari was nowhere to be seen.

Samar spotted Abha and went up to her. "Hey, Abha! How have you been?"

"I have been good. I am glad we had the same centre," replied Abha.

"Me too," he replied."I found the paper a bit tough. How about you?" asked Abha.

"It was not bad. Let's see," answered Samar. "So, where is your brother?"

"Rohit went to meet some friends at CP. He will come back later."

"That's great. Let's have some quick food at Gole Market."

After lunch, they walked back and sat in the park adjacent to the school, where many students sat in the shade of trees. Samar flipped through the *India Yearbook*. Abha was engrossed in her notes.

The next session, General Studies, resumed at 2.30 pm. The paper had 150 objective-type questions with four options each. Samar found the questions to be of varying type. Some answers were obvious, some were not, and for certain questions, he had no idea which option was correct, as he had never come across such information. These included:

Which one of them is a fish? a) Starfish b) Sea Horse c) Bombay Duck d) Cuttle fish.

Which one of the matches is/are not correct? a) Tel Aviv-Israel b) Bogota-Columbia c) Lima-Venezuela d) Dakar-Senegal.

What is the botanical name of Ashwagandha? a) *Rauwolffia serpentina* b) *Catharanthus tinctorius* c) *Tagetes floris* d) *Tectona grandis.*

How am I supposed to know so much? Leave It! It's better to attempt every question. I will try to keep the last 15 minutes for revision and rechecking.

He managed to do so and completed his paper comfortably before the final bell rang. The invigilators literally pulled the OMRs away from one or two candidates as they were still working on them.

Two police constables managed the crowd outside the main gate as the candidates exited. Samar was waiting for Abha outside the centre. She was among the last of the candidates to come out. She located Samar and walked towards him.

"How was this one?" Samar asked.

"It was so-so. How about you?" Abha asked in turn.

"So-so," Samar replied. "You copycat!" Abha punched him lightly on the arm.

"Shall we have a cup of coffee?" suggested Samar.

"Rohit has not arrived yet. So, yes! But we have to be quick."

They walked to the same coffee shop in the local market where they had eaten lunch earlier."When will you come back?" Samar posed the obvious question. "July. I spoke to my father, and he agreed," she smiled.

"Oh! That is about two months away."

"Yes. Meanwhile, can you ask the hostel owner to keep the same room ready from the 15th of July?" Abha requested.

"As you say, Madam!" Samar nodded happily.

"Let's go now. Rohit will throw a fit if he does not see me there," Abha said after their coffee was over.

"Your brother seems to be a pesky fellow!"

Abha made a face as they walked back to the centre. Samar wanted to spend more time together, but Abha saw her brother waiting for her. Rohit looked irritated.

"Where were you?"

"I just went for coffee and snacks. How was your meeting with your friends?"

"It was fine. Get in quickly. We have a long way to go."

Samar saw the Safari zoom past him while he was walking to the bus stand.

***

From the evening of the Prelims exam, aspirants shun their books for one or two weeks. They discuss the papers and try to solve them. The 'cut-off' becomes the buzzword. The coaching institutes solve the papers and declare the cut-off. The aspirants, after vigorous rounds of discussions and after consulting the solved papers of the coaching institutes, come out with their assessment of the cut-off for the particular year. GS and the optional subjects get their own cut-off every year. Experienced candidates act like 'experts' and 'consultants' on the cut-off marks. They predict results. Aspirants crossing the cut-off marks feel relieved, while those predicted to score below them feel anxious and disturbed.

It seemed both Samar and Sunny had fared well and were likely to clear the Prelims.

***

Sunny checked his result on the UPSC website. Within 30 seconds of entering his roll number, a message blinked on the screen:

CONGRATULATIONS! YOU HAVE QUALIFIED FOR THE CIVIL SERVICES (PRELIMINARY) EXAM!

Sunny banged his fist on the table. “I did it!” Samar closed his eyes as Sunny typed in his roll number. His heart thumped hard, and he felt he might faint.

CONGRATULATIONS! YOU HAVE QUALIFIED FOR THE CIVIL SERVICES (PRELIMINARY) EXAM!

“Aaj raat ki daaru party paaki!”

Sunny and Samar hugged each other euphorically. The other people in the cafe looked on in amusement. Sunny shouted the news to his parents and some friends over the PCO phone. Samar sat down and entered Abha’s roll number.

SORRY. YOUR ROLL NUMBER DOES NOT FIGURE IN THE LIST OF SUCCESSFUL CANDIDATES FOR THE CIVIL SERVICES (PRELIMINARY) EXAM!

Abha had failed to qualify! The bad news dampened Samar’s excitement. Sunny and Samar parted on the way back, Samar making his way towards Abha’s room. She had returned from Sonepat a week ago. They had resumed meeting each other, mostly in the evening.

How do I break the bad news?

I don’t want to break her heart.

She needed to clear this attempt. Will they allow her another attempt?

Abha was waiting for him, looking out from the window. As she came downstairs, Samar took her hands in his.

“Did you qualify?” Abha asked.

“Yes.” Samar nodded, though he looked away. He dreaded breaking the news to her.

“Did I qualify?”

Samar remained quiet.

“What is the matter? Did I fail?”

“Yes.”

Abha was stunned.

“I am so sorry,” Samar said feebly.

Abha stood in a stupor for a moment. Samar pulled her close to comfort her.

Abha broke down, hiding her face in his chest. "Abha, calm down." Samar patted her back.

She drew back abruptly.

Wiping her tears, she said, "Go and celebrate your success!"

"Abha… listen…"

"You shouldn't waste your precious time with me. Go and enjoy your day!"

"No *Babu*, listen to me. You can make it the next time."

"I am not your *Babu*! Please go!" Abha retorted.

Samar did not know how to console her.

Abha ran upstairs to her room and shut the door loudly. He called out, "Abha... Abha…"

There was no response.

It was as if his own dreams had been shattered.

Back at his place, he found Sunny in a discussion with a few students about how right they had been about the cut-off!

Sunny's friends had brought beer and *tandoori* chicken to celebrate.

Samar asked, "What is all this? This is the first time you have brought liquor here."

"I have refrained from drinking since I arrived in Delhi. But, today is a day to celebrate," Sunny shouted, lifting his beer bottle and pointing it towards his friends. They cheered loudly, "Yes! It's time to celebrate!"

"Come on! You must celebrate tonight," shouted one of Sunny's friends.

"No. I am good," Samar replied.

"No is not an option today," yelled one fellow.

Two of them caught hold of Samar and forced his mouth open, while Sunny poured beer into it. The others clapped and cheered.

"This is disgusting… so bitter!" Samar shouted over the loud cheers.

"*Hahaha*… Come on, it is not that bad," Sunny yelled.

"No. It's the elixir of life," shouted one boy. Others cheered loudly in agreement.

"Are you coming for a movie, champ?" offered Sunny.

"You people go ahead. I want to rest."

"Okay. You can skip the movie, but finish your beer!"

Samar somehow managed to finish his first bottle of beer.

An hour later, Sunny and his friends left for a late-night movie show. Left alone at home, Samar felt disturbed. He wanted to be with Abha, to hold her and console her.

Vipul came back very late after checking his result. He had failed to qualify, but he was cheerful. Udit also failed to qualify.

"Congratulations, Samar *bhai*!" said Vipul.

"Thank you. I am sorry, though."

"*Aaahhh,* no worries. I know I will clear it the next time."

Samar wished he could exchange his insecurities for Vipul's confidence.

***

The results were declared on the first Friday of August 2001. Abha planned to visit Sonepat four days later. Samar went to see her off. At the ISBT bus stand, Abha repeated the same rhetoric, "You should not waste your energy and time on failed aspirants."

"Abha, don't start all over again. I understand your pain, but what can we do? I am under immense pressure myself!" Samar replied.

"Don't pretend to be sorry for me, Samar. It's good for you. One competitor down!"

"Don't talk like that."

"Honestly, why should my failure affect you? I have to bear the consequences, not you! So stop acting as though you understand!"

Abha's sharp words hurt him. Her unreasonable behaviour was beyond his comprehension, but it prompted him to concentrate on his preparations. He immersed himself in the Mains preparations within a week after the Prelims results.

***

CHAPTER 6

Abha returned from Sonepat after a month. She somehow managed to convince her father to allow her one more attempt. She was also allowed to return to Delhi.

Rajan's classes had resumed for the Mains phase. Though they were for all aspirants of the batches that ended in March, they were attended mostly by those who had qualified for the Prelims. Samar and Sunny attended them regularly. The class ambience was much more serious now. The after-class discussions and group revisions were precise.

Samar had to choose his second option for the Mains exam. He had not paid much attention to it before the Prelims. Being a Political Science graduate, he had appeared in the Prelims with Public Administration as his optional, and that would remain his first optional. He consulted with Mr Ravi and a few other experienced aspirants. Mr Ravi advised him to choose a subject he found easy and which was high-scoring. Geography was a popular choice. Samar had found it easy and interesting during the Prelims preparation, so he decided on it. Geography was Sunny's optional, too.

Sunny had meticulously planned his UPSC preparations. He had completed the Geography coaching at Interactions in Mukherjee Nagar before joining Rajan's for Prelims coaching. He volunteered to share his Geography notes with Samar, which saved Samar time and money.

Vipul went home for a week and came back to resume his preparation for the next year's Prelims. He joined Psychology classes at Rajan's.

Samar and Sunny were engrossed in their Mains preparations. After about a fortnight, classes ended. The Mains examinations were scheduled for mid-October 2001.

***

Abha was happy she had got one more chance. She was also glad to be able to prolong the carefree life in Delhi, away from her family. Her mood improved as time passed. She visited Samar's flat once to inquire about his preparations and to convey her best wishes. Samar was unaffected by her visit as he wanted no distractions at this stage. Besides, her unreasonable behaviour during their last meeting was still fresh and painful.

About a month and a half after her return from Sonepat, Abha accidentally met Vinay Talwar, the property dealer. She was on her way to her hostel when Vinay called out to her, "Hello, Abha madam! How are things?"

"I am fine. How have you been, Vinay Ji? How is your property dealership going?"

"First class!" Vinay said, adding, "I hate to see you walking in the sun with so many bags."

"Just some shopping," she replied.

"Feel free to hop into my car. I can't bear to see such pretty hands carry so much weight!" Vinay flirted.

Abha got in, glad to get a lift.

"Before we head towards your hostel, would you care for some coffee or tea?" Vinay offered.

"No... No... I am fine. Just drop me at my hostel."

"Okay, as you say, Madam Ji."

After a minute, Vinay said, "Accha, Madam Ji... Tell me, when will you finally become an IAS?"

"Oh! It is a long process..." Abha sighed. "There are several stages: Prelims followed by Mains and an interview, and then the final result. If you clear it in a single attempt, it will take almost a year."

"Oh, my God! One year! That's a long period."

These small-town aspirants are really crazy. One year, just studying! Foolish people. Anyway, it's good that we get to make money from them.

"It needs a lot of perseverance, Vinay ji!"

"Hats off to all of you!" Vinay said. "Accha Madam ji, one of my cousins wants to meet an IAS aspirant for guidance. He has been pestering me for a while now."

"It seems the IAS bug bit him!"

"Something like that! Can I introduce him to you?" Vinay asked.

"There are so many others who are preparing. Like Samar. Do

you remember him? He can guide your cousin well. He has even cleared his Prelims," replied Abha.

"Oh, that Assamese boy! I remember him. But I think my cousin would prefer guidance from a pretty lady than from a dorky fellow!"

Abha hid her smile. The confidence with which Vinay flirted with her was amazing.

The car halted near her house.

"So, Madam Ji, shall I say yes from your side?"

"Okay. When does he want to meet?" Abha hopped out.

"Soon. I have the landline no. of your hostel. I will fix up a meeting with Punit."

"See you soon. Bye!"

***

The Mains examinations were 10 days away. Samar thoroughly revised his two optionals, Public Administration and Geography. The GS syllabus was vast, especially in current affairs, and time was limited. He revised his current affairs scrapbook, the magazine on current affairs, and rushed through the *India Yearbook,* but somehow lacked confidence. He feared he might have missed something inconsequential. Abha came by to convey her best wishes to Samar and Sunny.

The exam for General Studies I and II was held on the first day. It was common for all the candidates. Each paper was for 300 marks. Samar's exam centre was at a government school in Tilak Nagar, West Delhi. He attempted about 80 per cent of Part I and 75 per cent of Part II of GS.

Aspirants murmured amongst themselves as they headed out after the papers were over.

"UPSC lived up to its unpredictable Public Service Commission reputation."

"The papers were lengthy and unpredictable."

"How was that question about some war between some tribes in Africa important?"

"How could the UPSC ignore the US in the year 9/11 occurred?"

"I have heard of the *El Niño* effect, but what on earth is the *La Niña* effect?"

"UPSC is the number one enemy of aspirants."

Samar could not disagree!

The next two days covered Essays, English, and Hindi papers. The schedule of these exams, with no gap days, exhausted the candidates. Samar was not satisfied with his performance in the papers, but he tried to maintain his morale. There was a gap of a few days, and then the optional exams were held. They ended within 10 days. Sunny seemed hopeful about clearing the exams, but Samar was apprehensive and unhappy with his overall performance.

***

A month after Abha met Vinay, she received a call from him. "Punit is keen to meet you, Madam Ji!"

Dressed in a light-blue tube top and a navy-blue long skirt with hair loosely tied, Abha admired herself in the mirror before going downstairs.

Vinay was in the front seat of the black Mercedes C-Class sedan while Punit was at the wheel. Even though Vinay was trendily dressed, Abha found Punit to be dapper than his cousin. Dressed in a crisp white shirt and dark blue fitted jeans, Punit looked like a quintessential *Dilliwallah munda*.

"Let us head to a coffee shop somewhere, you both can discuss things there. Is it fine, Abha madam?" Vinay asked.

Punit pressed the accelerator without waiting for an answer, and the car zoomed past the crowded streets of Old Rajendra Nagar and onto the main road. Abha felt Punit's eyes on her through the rearview mirror. She found him easy on the eyes, with his clean-shaven, handsome face, prominent jawline, and light brown eyes.

"So, here we are at Maurya Sheraton. Have you been here before?" Vinay broke the silence.

"No," Abha replied.

They settled down at a cosy table in the cafe and ordered coffee.

"This is Punit, my brother from another mother! He has been telling me for a while that he wants to appear for IAS exams," said Vinay.

Taking a deep breath, he continued, "And now after seeing you, I fear he is sure of this crazy idea."

Abha found Vinay's flirtatious words audacious. "I wonder if your cousin has a voice," she said.

"Yes, he has a voice," Punit chuckled cheekily and continued, "Hello, I am Punit Oberoi. I passed out from Kirori Mal College."

Punit's deep voice was pleasant.

"Oh, I see. So, why IAS?" Abha asked.

"My entire family is involved in the garment export business. I am bored with mundane business routines and want to try something else."

Abha listened intently as the waiter served their order. "Good to hear that you want to carve a different path for yourself."

"You could say that. I was curious about this IAS thing. I read that lakhs of people from Bihar and UP come to Delhi to prepare for the IAS. I want to experience what it is!"

"That's interesting," said Abha.

"How do I start my preparation?" Punit asked eagerly.

"First, I suggest you join coaching classes. Rajan's is No.1 in the field."

"Is it the one where you took your coaching?"

"Yes. The batches are going to start soon."

"Okay. I will join the classes, but I need your guidance," Punit appealed.

"Definitely."

" Great! Is everything sorted now, bro?" Vinay patted Punit on his shoulder.

"Yes. I'm sorted and happy now."

Punit's infectious smile made her heart flutter with excitement.

***

A week later, Punit called Abha on the hostel phone. He wanted her help in buying reference books for UPSC preparation. Abha agreed to accompany him to Jia Sarai Market in South Delhi for the books.

On the appointed day, a red Honda CR-V startled Abha as it stopped abruptly, very close to where she was standing. The window pane rolled down, and Punit, wearing black goggles, flashed a smile.

"Were you planning to run me over?" Abha chided him as she got into the front seat.

"What to do? The excitement to meet you made me reckless!" teased Punit.

"Oh! That's too cheesy a line, but I am impressed, not with your cheesy line but with your swanky car."

"She is my current girlfriend!" Punit joked.

"She is a superb choice for a girlfriend," teased Abha.

"My girlfriend wants to go out on a ride. Shall we?"

"Yes, please. How can I annoy your girlfriend!"

Punit's confidence was as impressive as the red Honda CR-V. The car zoomed past the lanes of Rajendra Nagar with the latest Bollywood hits playing on the stereo.

"Have you been to Khan Market?" Punit asked.

"No. Where is it?" Abha enquired.

"It's a cool place. Let me take you there for coffee."

"Okay."

Khan Market was crowded; it housed many chic cafes and outlets. They found a cosy table in a posh cafe.

"This place has the best coffee in town," declared Punit. They ordered cappuccinos.

Khan Market impressed Abha with its ambience and kitschy outlets. It was very different from Rajendra Nagar, young girls flaunting the latest trends, smartly dressed expats, and fashionably dressed middle-aged ladies in cashmere shawls.

Abha enjoyed the outing. It was a welcome change from the mundaneness of studies. They spent over three hours at the cafe and a few more window shopping and walking around the alleys, flirting and smiling.

"I am afraid we will have to visit Jia Sarai on another occasion," said Punit.

"I think you made up the whole Jia Sarai trip," Abha teased.

"No, my girlfriend did. She wanted to drive you to these fancy places," Punit chuckled.

"Thank you, Punit's girlfriend," said Abha, patting the side door of the SUV.

When they reached her hostel, Punit presented her with a box of imported assorted chocolate truffles. "Thank you so much. See you soon." After reaching her room, Abha reflected on the evening and how much she had enjoyed it. In Sonepat, she lived in the shadow of her family and their imposed restrictions. She envied the young girls in Khan Market for their freedom.

***

Once the Mains were over, Samar and Sunny planned a short trip to the *Vaishno Devi* shrine. A few of Sunny's friends also joined them.

The trip was a brief, refreshing break for the boys. Soon after returning from the trip, Samar's mood improved. He took up local tuitions for three hours a day and gradually increased his study hours for the Prelims next year. He wanted to revive the old study group and also reconnect with Abha. They had hardly talked during the Mains phase. The study group would be a good way to rekindle his relationship with her. Samar had decided to forget her harsh words. He missed her.

One day, about a fortnight after the trip, he strolled to her hostel around 11 am and called out for her.

Abha peeped out of the window. "Hi!"

Samar took a while to respond as his eyes lingered on her. "Hi, Abha. Can you come downstairs?"

"Okay."

She came down after about five minutes.

"Hi. What is it? I am surprised to see you today," Abha said with a faint smile.

"I was away. I had gone to *Vaishno Devi*. I have brought you some *prasad*."

Samar handed her a small bag with *prasad* from the shrine.

"Thank you. Yes, I heard you went with Sunny and some boys."

"So, how are you doing?"

"I am fine. I am trying to concentrate on the Prelims. How was your Mains?" she asked.

"They were so-so. Let's see. I have begun my Prelims preparation, too."

"That's good."

Abha's response was mechanical. He could sense that something had changed.

"I was wondering, should we resume our study group?" Samar suggested hesitantly.

"My family has given me just one last chance. I think group studies tend to waste a lot of time. I am not keen on it."

"Oh! Maybe we can study together."

"That is also not possible," Abha said apologetically. "I prefer only self-study. Besides, where would we assemble?"

"At my place. We can study there."

"I am afraid that is not a good idea. I don't want to visit the boys' flats. People notice, you know."

Samar realized there was no point in trying to convince Abha. She had changed. She had not hesitated to visit his place or go out with him until a few months ago.

"Okay. Do you want to grab lunch together?"

"Not today. Maybe next time."

"All right then, study well. See you another time."

Abha shook hands with him. "I am sorry to have disappointed you," she said.

"No… No… I understand."

The companionship and closeness they had shared until a few months ago was markedly absent. The intervening period during the Mains changed their relationship.

Samar made his way to a nearby park with a heavy heart. He felt they had drifted apart with no possibility of return. Love could not bear the burden of circumstances in their lives. Tears rolled down his cheeks, and he was glad the park was almost empty at that odd hour. He blamed himself, oblivious of Punit's entry in Abha's life.

***

CHAPTER 7

Rajan's IAS Study Circle was abuzz with admission activities for new batches. Punit was able to join one of the batches.

Classes commenced in full swing. Punit drove to classes from home, unlike most Delhi aspirants, who used public transport or motorcycles. Most other students did not take him seriously, probably because of his swanky, expensive cars.

He's not a serious aspirant; he's just a show-off, a typical dumb Delhiite from an affluent background!

His joint family was quite amused at his decision to try for the IAS. The elders thought it was a temporary phase that would pass.

"Bache ko apni mann ki karne do!"

For Punit, it was a welcome change. He was enjoying the new daily routine. Almost every evening after classes, he would meet Abha for coffee in the neighbourhood or in some other fancy cafe in CP or Khan Market. This was the highlight of the day for both of them. Their mutual attraction was evident. Samar's love looked pale, poor, and pathetic compared to Punit's company, flirtations, and gifts. Punit loved spending time with an attractive girl, while Abha felt special. In the process, she was losing focus on her primary goal, the UPSC exam.

***

The Mains results were declared on the Friday of the second week of March. The roll numbers of the successful candidates were listed on the official UPSC website. Sunny cleared the Mains stage, but Samar was unsuccessful.

Samar felt disheartened for a few days and took a fortnight to recover. He met Mr Ravi and his teachers at Rajan's, who motivated him to learn from his failures and bounce back. This encouraged him to gear up for the next attempt. Three weeks after the Mains results, he received a postcard from his brother, Amar, urging him to visit home.

Samar reluctantly boarded the Brahmaputra Mail to Guwahati. He hated visiting Guwahati at this stage because he dreaded his sister-in-law's mocking face for failing the Mains. He was right. Although Maloti hardly said anything, he could hear her silent, mocking jibes.

That evening after dinner, Amar came to Samar's room to show a notice from the Land Acquisition Collector. Samar sat up in bed.

"See this… It is a declaration under Section 6 of the Land Acquisition Act." Amar handed over the paper to Samar.

"Our house is going to be acquired. They are expanding the highway. The house is still registered in our father's name. We are the legal heirs, so it entitles us to the compensation," he explained.

The sudden developments perturbed Samar as they were not conducive to his future plans. It meant they would have to vacate the house in a few months.

"Anyway, you must be exhausted. Take rest now. We will discuss the matter tomorrow," Amar concluded.

The next day, Samar and Amar were silently eating lunch. Maloti kept looking at Amar, unhappy with him for not discussing the compensation matter. Halfway through the meal, Samar raised the issue.

"What next, *Dada*?"

"Samar, we need to get the ownership mutated to our names."

"Okay."

"We need to submit the legal heirship application to the SDO's office."

Maloti, who was serving food, retorted, "Your brother is unable to spell out the entire issue, Samar."

"Maloti, you don't need to intervene. I will handle it."

"I know how well you handle it," Maloti snapped at Amar. "For once, let me spell out the things clearly." Amar fiddled with his spoon while Maloti spoke, "Samar, you know how much we sacrificed for your studies and future. Your brother does not have a high-paying job of a Collector," Maloti said. "Abhimanyu is growing up, and his expenses are increasing."

Samar could not comprehend, but he had a hunch something guileful was coming up. He became alert as he picked up a morsel of *daal*-soaked rice.

Maloti modulated her voice to a softer tone, "Surely, you would want to repay some of our sacrifices?"

"I will repay everything someday, *Nobau*. I will!" murmured Samar, gulping a mouthful of water.

"Why not now then? God has given you an opportunity. You can relinquish your share to your brother."

So, this was the sly plan in Maloti's mind. Or perhaps in Amar da's mind, too!

Samar stopped eating and glanced at Amar, who avoided his eyes, looking downwards."You mean a Relinquishment Deed?"

"This is your turn to repay us for the money and all the years of sacrifice we spent on you," Maloti suggested to Samar, in a soft, sly, artful voice. It amused him how she could shift from a harsher to a softer tone in the flash of a second, depending on the situation.

Samar was dismayed that his brother was supporting this proposition, even if indirectly. "What are you thinking, Samar? The compensation will not be that high. It would hardly be a few lakhs. Your father did not leave a vast fortune, you know," Maloti ridiculed.

"Maloti, enough! You better mind your language," Amar roared, pointing his index finger at her.

"Why should I? Did I say anything wrong? What did your father leave for us? Only this brother of yours to fend for! Such a poor, disgusting family! Always in penury!"

Amar lost control over his anger at the insult. He got up and slapped her. The slap was powerful enough to send Maloti sprawling onto the floor. "*Hai Bhagavaan!* Why don't you kill me right now? My life was ruined the day I got married into this household," Maloti shrieked, beating the floor with her fists.

She then started beating her forehead and screamed, "*Marile oo! Marile oo! Morilo oo! Morilo oo!*" (He hit me! He hit me! I am going to die! I am going to die!)

The brothers did not know what to do or how to react. Pointing a finger at Samar, Maloti shouted, "Get out of here, you scoundrel! You are the reason for all this!"

Samar left the house in disgust. Amar called out to him, but he did not respond. He could hear the howls of his sister-in-law till the turning at the end of the street.

After wandering around aimlessly for hours, he returned very late at night. A lull had set in the house after the melodrama of the evening. Samar went straight to his room and lay down on his bed. After a while, Amar came into his room.

"I am really sorry, Samar," Amar whimpered. He folded his hands and started to bend down to touch Samar's feet.

"Dada, what are you doing? Don't do this, please!"

Samar caught hold of Amar's hands and pulled him up. He made Amar sit beside him.

"I know Maloti has always been unfair towards you," Amar lamented incoherently. "She has threatened to leave me and take Abhimanyu to her parents' place."

"Dada, don't cry," Samar consoled him. After about a minute, Amar gathered himself, wiping away his tears, and said, "I am very sorry, brother. I have been unfair to you. You had to take up tuition during your college days, as I could barely support you with my meagre income."

"You have done your best, Dada." Samar held Amar's right hand and said, "*Nobau* is right. It is time to pay it back. I don't have any money to pay you back, so relinquishing my share is the only option."

"No… No…" Amar stood up, his body shaking.

Samar said calmly, "Do not worry, Dada. I will be fine. I have taken up tuitions in Delhi and will support my expenses."

"It is not fair to you."

Tears rolled down Amar's cheeks. Samar held back his tears.

The next day, they went to the SDO's office and filed the legal heirship and Samar's relinquishment application.

Things were back to normal at the house. That afternoon, Maloti cooked Samar's favourite dishes and took special care in serving them to him.

Samar left for Delhi the next day. The new developments at home, his sister-in-law's attitude, and his predicament strengthened his resolve to clear the UPSC exam. He was penniless and without any backup now.

***

One weekend, about four months after Punit joined classes, Abha received a call from him on the hostel line at around 9:30 pm. "Hey, have you been to a discotheque?" asked Punit.

"No. Never!" Abha answered.

"Never mind. I am coming in an hour. Be ready."

Abha rummaged frantically through her bags for a suitable outfit. She hardly had any Western outfits. She selected a tight-fitting, dark maroon satin top and a black knee-length skirt. With deep red lipstick, mascara, and eye shadow, she looked set for the evening.

Punit was dressed in a casual party shirt and dark blue jeans.

"I did not know IAS people dressed like this," Punit commented admiringly, as he opened the front door of the Honda CR-V for Abha.

"What do you mean? Am I not appropriately dressed?" Abha asked as she climbed into the front seat.

"You are dressed perfectly for the occasion!" Punit closed the door and got in.

"I had limited options," Abha replied coyly. Punit ran his eyes over her and touched her face momentarily. His fingers tantalized her smooth cheeks.

"Let's party then!" he announced loudly.

He pressed the accelerator, and the black CR-V zoomed its way through the main road. The drive was smooth with scanty traffic. They arrived at the porch of The Ashok in 20 minutes and left the SUV for the valet to park.

The ambience at the discotheque entrance was new to Abha. There was a crowd of young people. Some flaunted the latest trends, while some looked overdressed in their expensive designer dresses. Some girls wore skimpy outfits, indifferent to the cold January weather. They were all waiting to gain entry, a privilege reserved for the fortunate and exclusive. Punit, familiar with the grind, waved at the bouncer manning the entrance, who signalled him to come forward. Punit took Abha's hand and made his way through the crowd. The bouncer greeted them and stamped their forearms. As Punit pulled her inside, Abha glanced back at the other unfortunate ones with pride, glad to be one of the exclusive ones.

Punit made his way to the bar where he met some friends.

"Scotch for the gentleman. What will the pretty lady have, Sir?" the friendly bartender asked loudly.

Abha had no clue about cocktails as she had never had one.

"A Mojito for the pretty lady," Punit shouted at the bartender over the blaring music.

Abha took a sip. The tantalizing taste of the Mojito was refreshing. She looked around her. The club was dimly lit, and the DJ played the latest international hits. Disco lights were dancing from one end to the other, covering the entire space. Some people were grooving on the disco floor, while others were talking loudly in small groups.

A skimpily dressed girl tripped over Punit's foot, probably intentionally.

"Who is this girl?" she asked, looking at Abha with mocking eyes. Punit ignored her.

"Why are you ignoring me?" The girl whisked her finger over Punit's cheek while she swayed to the music.

"Ria, you are drunk." Punit steadied her.

"Is she prettier than me, *bolo... bolo*?" Ria clutched at his arm to stay steady.

"Ria, are you here with friends or alone?"

"Is she better than me?"

"Behave yourself, Ria," Punit scolded her.

Another girl arrived at the scene and took Ria away.

"I don't like her!" Ria blabbered on her way.

Punit looked embarrassed. "I apologize for her behaviour."

"You two seem close." Abha looked perturbed.

"I know her. We dated a long time back. But we broke up as she was not loyal. Anyway, I am sorry again."

"It's okay. You do not owe me any explanation. I am not your girlfriend."

"Still, what she said is not right. I don't like such girls. They have no control," Punit paused and continued, "But you are a sweet, decent girl. You don't have any vices."

"How do you know that?" Abha teased.

"I just know. Anyway, do you want to try a new drink, maybe a Bloody Mary?"

"Okay."

The foot-tapping music, the refreshing cocktails, and the new experience revived Abha's spirits.

"Come on, let's go to the dance floor," Punit invited her.

"I don't know how to dance."

"Come on. Just sway and shake your body. That's it." Punit slipped his hand around her waist and pulled her to the floor.

Initially, she hesitated in her steps, but at his encouragement, she relaxed. The heady mix of cocktails in her system hit her, and she threw her arms around his neck and clung to him, hiding herself in his chest. Punit pulled her tightly to him. He was an expert in handling girls in such situations. He led her to a corner stand and ordered more drinks. Three hours passed. Finally, the DJ stopped the music. It was closing time.

In about 20 minutes, the car was on the street outside Abha's hostel. The main gate was locked. Abha tried calling Richa, the girl in the room next to hers with Punit's phone, but she did not get any response. There was no way she could get inside the hostel.

"It's my fault. I should have told you no inmate is allowed in past 11.30 pm," Abha said.

"Don't worry, Abha. Trust me. I will arrange something," Punit responded.

Abha looked worried. She was stranded outside her hostel on a cold night, but Punit's presence reassured her.

Punit dialled Vinay's cell.

"*Vinay bhai! Ek room arrange hoga abhi?*"

"*Tere liye toh jaan bhi hazeer hain, mere veerey!*"

Vinay arranged a hotel room in Karol Bagh through his links. The three-star hotel room had a double bed. The situation was awkward for them, but there was no option.

"It's very late, so I think we should sleep now," said Punit.

"Yes, but I have a bit of a headache."

"Lie down and close your eyes. You will feel better," Punit's voice was reassuring.

They tossed and turned, but sleep evaded them. The sexual tension between them was palpable. Punit turned towards her, lightly touched her face with his fingers and asked, "May I ask you a personal question? I hope you will not get offended."

"I won't be offended," Abha replied, eyes still closed.

" Are you… a… I mean… a virgin?"

"What do you think?"

"I think you are a virgin."

Abha opened her eyes and looked at Punit. They stared at each other in the dark. Punit's fingers touched her trembling lips. Abha slid her palm over Punit's back. They pulled each other close and lost themselves in the throes of passion.

There was no guilt or regret the next morning. Abha felt as if she had entered a new chapter in her life. Punit had opened a new realm of pleasures she had not known before.

"Stop devouring me with your eyes," Punit teased, putting on his shirt. Abha's eyes were fixed on his muscular chest and toned abs.

"I was trying to capture your image to remember these moments forever," Abha replied, still lying in bed, white sheets covering her naked body.

"I was thinking you were undressing me with your eyes!" Punit teased.

Abha threw a pillow at him.

The previous night's encounter was the first of many such nights.

***

CHAPTER 8

The final results of the 2001 civil services exam were declared in the second week of May 2002. Sunny had performed well in his interview and was confident about his result. Samar accompanied him to check the results put up on the UPSC bulletin board. Sunny secured the 107th rank. They embraced each other euphorically. There were boisterous celebrations around the bulletin board window by successful candidates and their friends. The ones who had failed tried to conceal their dejection.

The visit to UPSC and the joy and relief of the successful candidates strengthened Samar's willpower and boosted his determination. He followed a strict regimen of studies and revision. Amar sent him money occasionally. His sister-in-law did not raise any objection after the relinquishment deed was filed. Amar told him that the compensation amount received for the house was a few lakhs.

I have no financial backing left, and clearing the exam is my only option to secure my future.

Samar motivated himself with such thoughts.

Finally, D-Day arrived. The ambience at the exam centre was no different from the last time. But Samar was more confident this time. He was satisfied with his second Prelims attempt, as was Vipul, his flatmate.

Abha and Punit had the same centre as they had submitted their forms together. Both thought they performed well in the exam.

Sunny stayed back for about a month after the results. During this time, he visited his native place. He completed the formalities for joining the Foundation Course at the Lal Bahadur Shastri National Academy of Administration, popularly known as LBSNAA, in Mussoorie. He was allotted the Indian Police Service.

UPSC declared the results for Prelims 2002 in the third week of July. Samar went to Dholpur House to check the results. He cleared the exam, and so did Vipul and Udit.

Samar saw Abha there with Punit. Samar had heard that Abha was dating someone. He felt a tug in his heart, but the joy and relief of clearing the Prelims overshadowed the heartache.

Both Abha and Punit failed to qualify the Prelims. Abha broke down, her tears flowing freely.

"Calm down, Abha," Punit's words offered little consolation to her. "What will I do now? My family will take me away from here," Abha wailed.

"Don't worry. I won't let them." Punit put his arm around her.

"You don't know my family," Abha's sobbing made her words almost incoherent.

"The world will not end, Abha. There is life beyond the UPSC!"

"I wanted to prove that I can stand on my own feet! My dreams are shattered now," she said piteously.

Samar wanted to console her, but he hesitated. She had given away that right to someone else.

Punit steadied her, and they left, Abha leaning on him.

Punit was unaffected by the result. For him, it was merely an experiment that had failed.

"It is not a big deal. I will return to my family business. Besides, the entire UPSC exercise is too long," Punit justified to Vinay later.

For his family, it was like, *"Bacche ne apne mann ki kar lee na... Koi nai! Aab laut aaya! Der aaye, durust aaye!"*

***

This can't be happening!

The strip showed a positive pregnancy test.

What am I going to do? How did I get pregnant?

If my family finds out, they will kill me.

Punit will sort everything out! There's no need to panic!

Abha had missed her period about a fortnight after the Prelims results came out. She was puzzled because Punit had claimed to have used protection every time they made love. She felt she could not breathe as she anxiously waited for Punit to arrive that evening.

"Punit, I have tested positive," she said in a low voice as they sat across the table in a neighbourhood coffee shop.

Punit looked bemused.

"I am pregnant!"

"What? What do you mean?" Punit yelled.

"I said, I am pregnant. Keep your voice down, please," Abha said in a hushed tone.

"Are you sure it's mine?" Punit controlled himself.

"What do you mean? I have never slept with anyone else!" said Abha agitatedly. She glanced around to see if anyone had overheard her.

"Okay. Okay… I am sorry. I mean, I always use protection. Don't worry, we will figure it out."

"How? What will you do? My family will burn me alive if they find out!" she said, her heart thumping hard.

Punit was extremely upset. He had slept with many women but had not encountered such a situation.

"We will plan what to do. Don't worry and calm down."

Punit did not stay much longer that evening. His family had been urging him to join the family business. The IAS bug had subsided since the Prelims results. He had no patience to attempt the civil services exam again.

She seems to be the clingy type. I have to get rid of her.

I should stop meeting these small-town girls. They overreact.

Abha pondered over her situation and its consequences. Her family had given her one last opportunity, but she had failed. The immediate result would be that they would force her to return to Sonepat. The subject of marriage would come up once again.

I must convince Punit to marry me. I am sure he will.

I know he loves me.

You are a fool, Abha! He does not love you.

No, he does. You will see.

Marriage with him will come with freedom, a big city lifestyle, and money to spend…

***

"Will you marry me?" asked Abha as soon as she met Punit, a week after she tested positive.

"Are you serious?"

"Yes, I am serious. I love you, Punit. You love me too, don't you?"

"What is this nonsense?" Punit snapped.

"Are you calling my love nonsense?"

"Can you stop this melodrama?" Punit's face was red with anger.

"You know how much I love and adore you. You are the first and last person to touch me!" Abha pleaded.

"When did I say I love you? We love to spend time together, that's it," Punit retorted.

Abha was shocked at his reaction. "You said you love me a few times… You know, when we were… in bed."

"That was in the heat of the moment. How can you take those words literally?"

"What? What do you mean, Punit?"

"I am confused. I don't know whether I love you or not, but I can't marry you. I need to set my foothold in the family business."

"We have shared such lovely moments. Let us treasure them for our entire lives! Let's bring this child into this world!"

Abha tried to hold his hand, but Punit pulled his hand away.

"Punit, try to understand my situation. I am a girl. My reputation is at stake."

"Stop this drama!" Punit almost shouted.

Abha was distraught by his response. He seemed to be a completely different person.

"Nothing will happen to your reputation. I have a plan," Punit said, controlling himself.

Abha looked at him numbly.

"I will take you to an abortion clinic. Don't worry. I will bear all the expenses. No one will know," Punit reassured her.

"You are not making any sense to me," Abha said.

There was silence for a while.

Then Abha said quietly, "I am ready to give you some time to think. Think about our good times. I am sure we will be happy together… I love you so much…" Tears trickled down her face.

"Are you sure you love me and not my stuff?" Punit mocked. "You love my car, my money, going to fancy places, and the freedom and attention you get. Don't try to fool me, Abha. I know you well. You don't love me."

"You are hurting my feelings, Punit," Abha sobbed, shocked at his words.

"If you do not stop this drama, I swear, I will walk out right now," Punit warned.

See, I told you. He does not love you. He used you!

"How do I prove that I love you?" Abha asked through her sobs.

Punit got up abruptly, muttering some curse words to himself, and walked off.

"Punit… Punit! Please don't go. Listen, please!" Abha pleaded. She became conscious of the people around who had witnessed the embarrassing scene between them. Some were familiar aspirants.

Punit got into his car and zoomed off, leaving Abha standing in the street, looking after him.

Abha's heart and mind were conflicted.

What a fool I was! All this time, he was using me.

What about you? Were you not also using him?

You went to fancy pubs and dined at posh restaurants. You got pampered and received expensive gifts. In exchange, he slept with you. It was a simple transaction!

But I loved him.

You did not love him. You loved the idea of loving him!

What a fool I was to have trusted him. I should have trusted Samar. He loved me. It was a mistake to shun him.

You thought you had a better option in Punit. He was a rich Dilliwallah! That's why you dumped Samar.

***

Two days later, Samar had come for a quick coffee break when he saw Punit and Abha sitting together in a local cafe across the road. Abha appeared to be pleading and trying to convince Punit, who seemed irritated and agitated. Samar could gauge that things were not right between them.

After Punit sped off in his car, Samar went over to Abha, who looked distraught. She was horrified that he may have witnessed everything and tried to look away.

"Stop crying, Abha," he said comfortingly.

"We just broke up," Abha sobbed.

"I am sorry to hear that," Samar said. "Probably it's for the best. He does not deserve you."

It took Abha a while to gather herself. Samar stood by her side, patting the back of her head softly.

***

A week later, Punit took Abha to an obscure private clinic for an abortion... Afterwards, he dropped her off outside her hostel. They hardly spoke to each other.

While parting, Punit said, "I am sorry if I hurt you, Abha. This is our last meeting. All the best for your future."

She hated him at that moment, and her pent-up emotions burst out as she got out of the car. "I don't want your best wishes! I don't want to see your face again! I hate you!" she screamed at him. "You used me… I hate you."

"You used me and my money, too!" Punit smirked.

"Get lost!"

Punit zoomed off, fuming with anger.

She shouted after him, "You are a bastard!"

That was the last time they saw each other.

***

CHAPTER 9

Ten days after her abortion, Abha turned up at Samar's doorstep. Dusk had set in. Samar was surprised to see her. She looked weak and tired.

"Hi, Abha… Come on in."

"Hi! I hope everything is well with you."

"Yes. Just concentrating on my upcoming Mains."

"That's great…" Abha was struggling to find the right words. "I came to apologize to you. I wanted to come earlier, but I had to visit Sonepat. I returned yesterday."

Samar did not respond.

"I am extremely sorry for everything."

There was a momentary pause as Abha struggled to control her emotions. Then she said, "You have been caring and helpful. I was so foolish!"

Samar looked uncomfortable.

"I am sure you remember all the good times we had together," Abha said. "How did we drift apart, Samar?"

He remained silent.

"I regret that I trusted Punit. He is such a jerk!"

Samar muttered, "Punit seems to be an arrogant fellow with loads of attitude and a superiority complex."

"I have realized my mistake and misjudgement. I behaved rudely with you," Abha recited the rehearsed lines perfectly.

"You did not misbehave. Maybe you thought of him as a better option," Samar said, clearing his throat.

"I chose the wrong person…" her voice choked.

She caught his right hand and said softly, "You and I had such a beautiful relationship, but it withered away. I want to reconnect and start afresh." Abha gazed into his eyes, seeking his reaction.

Samar looked into her eyes. She looked genuine.

Abha said, "Let bygones be bygones. It's great news that you have qualified for the Mains." Then she added, cajolingly, "I was wondering if we could watch *Devdas*. I heard it is good."

Samar agreed, and they took a rickshaw to Liberty Cinema

Hall that evening. The tickets were all sold out at the counter, but they managed to get two tickets in black.

In the movie hall, about half an hour into the film, Abha rested her head on Samar's shoulder. The familiar feelings crept in. After a while, she caught his left hand in hers and squeezed it. Samar's heart thumped hard.

After the movie, they went to Popular Dhaba, like the old times. On their way back to her hostel, Abha pulled him close and hugged him.

The evening ended on a happy note. Abha's family had forced her to abandon UPSC aspirations. They insisted on her getting married. Talks were on with the families of a few potential grooms. It was a Herculean task for Abha to convince her family to let her return to Delhi for a while. They had imposed a precondition that she would have to wind up her affairs and return within a fortnight.

What should I do?

She decided to make amends with Samar.

He is dependable! And he still cares for me!

***

The deadline set by Abha's family was fast approaching. Abha was panicky and rushed to Samar. He was alone at home.

"I need your help, Samar. Please…" Abha pleaded at the doorstep. He ushered her in. Abha was dishevelled and distraught. She looked like she had spent a few sleepless nights.

"What is the matter?" Samar asked.

"Can you take me away from here? I don't want to go back to Sonepat!" Abha said hysterically as they entered the living room.

"Calm down…"

Samar poured a glass of water and offered it to her as she sat down.

"They are coming this weekend. They are planning to marry me off. They will not even take my consent," Abha said incoherently.

"They can't marry you off without your consent," Samar replied.

"You don't know my family. They can go to any extent, even kill me if need be!"

He saw genuine fear in her eyes and patted her arm. "Okay… Calm down."

"Please take me away to a safer place."

"Where? I have my Mains examinations coming up in less than two months!"

"Anywhere… maybe we can run away to Shimla or Dehradun or even the Northeast. Why not Guwahati? The Northeast would be far, far safer…"

"It is not that simple. You don't know how crucial it is for me to clear the exam this time. I don't want to get disturbed emotionally."

Abha gathered herself and said, "I am sorry. I am being selfish, dragging you into my problem. This is a matter of life and death for me. I thought you loved me and would support me."

"Don't take this the wrong way. I care for you and your happiness. You don't know how much it hurt me when you abandoned me…" Samar's pent-up emotions flowed freely. He turned his back towards Abha, struggling to hold back his tears.

Abha caught him from behind, clinging tightly.

"I wish we could spend our lives together!" she said softly.

Samar looked into her eyes.

She looks so vulnerable, wronged, and defeated.

Overwhelmed with emotion, Samar pulled her close to him and kissed her softly on the lips. She responded immediately, parting her lips. She caressed his wavy dark hair…

After some time, Samar said, "Let me think about what I can do for you, my love."

Abha left after half an hour.

Samar did not know whom to approach for help and advice. Vipul opined that he was being manipulated and advised him to concentrate on his Mains exam preparations. Samar rang up Sunny, who was at LBSNAA. Sunny offered them a place in Chandigarh to hide but suggested delaying any such move till the coming weekend. He was coming to Chandigarh from LBSNAA over the weekend.

Things did not turn out as planned.

Abha came rushing to Samar's flat three days later, knocking at the door frantically. It was afternoon, and Samar was taking a power nap. The loud thumping at the door downstairs interrupted his sleep. Irritated, he went down to see who it was.

"Samar! Samar! Please take me away from here now!" Abha babbled hysterically.

Samar struggled to keep his eyes wide open. But he saw real fear in her eyes.

"What happened?" Samar caught hold of her.

"My brother and cousin are on their way from Sonepat to take me away!"

"Calm down. Let us talk upstairs."

Stumbling into the living room, she said, "Samar… they will be here soon…"

"Don't panic, Abha. I will talk to them and request them not to force you into anything without your consent."

"You don't know them."

"There must be some solution, baby!"

"Do you think I am dramatizing things? Please help me. I will always be indebted to you. I know I am asking too much. You have exams… I have no one else to ask for help…" Abha folded her hands and pleaded, fear and anxiety choking her voice. She sank to the floor.

Samar pulled her up and led her to a chair. He handed her a glass of water and said, "Let me think."

Samar pondered the situation. On one hand, his exams were approaching, and on the other hand, Abha needed support. It was a critical situation for her.

A quick plan was hatched. They packed their bags in less than an hour. Sunny told Samar to rent a taxi to take them to Chandigarh, where his servant would receive them and help them lie low for a while. Thereafter, they would plan the future course of action. Abha contacted Vinay Talwar to book a taxi. He also operated taxi tours as a side business.

It was midnight when they reached the address in Zirakpur, on the outskirts of Chandigarh. Sunny's servant, Moti Lal, was waiting for them at the hideout, which was a hut in the fields with some basic provisions. He left after handing them the keys.

The room had a thatched roof and smelt musty as though it had remained locked for a long time. The walls were mouldy, with cobwebs hanging from them. There was hardly any furniture, except for a *charpoy* and an old, dust-laden teakwood table and chair.

Abha dusted the bedsheet twice and spread it on the bed. After they washed their faces, they lay down side by side on the uncomfortable *charpoy*, exhausted from the quick turn of events. It was very cold, and they slept fitfully.

The next morning, they ate the cold food from the previous night, pondering over the next step. They had around Rs 18,000 between them.

"Abha, what should we do next?" Samar asked. "We cannot remain here for more than two or three days."

"My close friend, Aarti, stays in Shimla with her husband. I will stay with her for a while and figure out what to do. You can drop me off there and return to Delhi," Abha replied, staring at the wall.

"That sounds like a good plan," Samar agreed. *He would first drop her off safely in Shimla...*

Samar had taken out the *charpoy* into the courtyard to soak in the warmth of the sunshine. He looked anxious. Abha came over and patted him on the shoulder, saying, "I am sorry for all this mess. You need to get back to studying for the Mains."

"It's fine. That's what friends are for."

"Samar, I am terrified. Can you hold me for a while?" Abha asked.

Samar extended his arms to hold her. She clutched at him, fearful of him leaving her alone. They closed their eyes and rested. Within half an hour, both fell asleep. There was silence and solitude all around...

***

A loud thud at the wooden door startled them awake. Someone pushed against the door to open it.

"Open up! Is there anyone in there?"

They looked at each other with fear in their eyes. The intruder kicked the rickety door harder to force it open. Samar shouted, "Who is it?"

"Open the door!"

It was not Moti Lal's voice. Something was not right. Samar looked around and found a shovel lying idle on the ground. He picked it up and put it across the clutch to block the door from opening. Abha rushed inside the room and hid under the table. She was shivering with fear. The forceful kicks on the old rickety door grew harder.

"Open the door!"

Samar waited, unable to decide what to do. The kicks became more forceful. The rusted metallic clutch of the door caved in, and the door flung open, swinging to and fro from the assault.

Four sturdy goons barged in, followed closely by Rohit and another young fellow. Abha peeped from under the table. She was stunned to see her brother and her cousin, Atul. Rohit stepped towards the room where Abha was hiding. Samar rushed to block his way. Rohit caught Samar by the neck and banged him savagely against the wall, shouting, "What did you think, we can't find you?"

The rough assault caused Samar to bleed from his nose. Two goons surrounded him, and one punched him in the stomach.

Abha shrieked as Rohit dragged her out of the room.

"Don't do this! Please don't do this!" Abha yelled.

"Why didn't you come home?" Rohit shouted.

He clasped her chin roughly. Atul caught hold of her from behind.

"I don't want to go home! Leave me! Leave me!" Abha shouted, struggling to escape their clutches.

"Why did you run away with this joker?"

"I don't want to get married right now."

Rohit slapped her so hard that her face jerked backwards.

"Leave her alone! Let us discuss things!" Samar shouted.

"Shut up, you bastard!" Rohit snarled at Samar. The goons laughed savagely.

Rohit and Atul dragged Abha to the exit. The goons released

Samar. Abha was struggling to break free, screaming, "Help me... Help me... Samar!"

Samar pushed Rohit and Atul so hard they fell to the side, freeing Abha. She ran towards the door. One goon grabbed Abha, while two restrained Samar.

"You bastard!" screamed Rohit. "I will kill you, right here, right now!"

He punched and kicked Samar several times with brutal force. Blood gushed out of Samar's nose and mouth. Then Atul kicked him in the stomach.

"Leave him alone! Please leave him alone!" Abha pleaded, screaming.

Rohit picked up the shovel and banged Samar on the head savagely. The assault was so brutal that Samar lost consciousness and sank to the ground. Rohit kicked him again on his chest, arms, and face.

"Stop it! Don't hurt him!" Abha screamed.

"Get inside the car, or I will kill this joker!" Rohit yelled.

"Stop! Stop! For God's sake! I will come!" Abha wailed.

Rohit gave one final heavy kick to Samar's face.

The goons picked up Abha's belongings. They tied her hands, put her in the back seat of the Innova parked outside, and sped off.

***

CHAPTER 10

Moti Lal found Samar in a semi-conscious state, bleeding profusely. He was rushed to PGI, Chandigarh.

"He has suffered a hairline skull fracture. His brain scan was normal—no internal bleeding. But I am afraid there is a serious compound fracture in the right arm. We have to operate on it," the doctor briefed Sunny, who had rushed to Chandigarh.

Samar regained consciousness a few hours after being admitted and underwent surgery.

"It will take about 12 weeks for the bones of the arm to join. Until then, eat, sleep, and heal!" the doctor advised.

Amar arrived in Chandigarh two days after the incident. They kept Samar under observation in the ICU for two days and discharged him a week later. Amar took Samar to Delhi to collect his belongings and books. Thereafter, they booked their flight tickets to Guwahati.

Back in Guwahati, the ugly incident—the miseries, the atrocities, the injustice, and his failure to protect her—haunted Samar. He suffered from mood swings. His heart was miserable for Abha and his hopeless situation. He was angry with himself for ruining his Mains attempt.

Amar and Abhimanyu's care helped Samar recover. His sister-in-law took every opportunity to mock him, "Look what our IAS aspirant did! Instead of chasing his dreams, he chased skirts."

The 12-week-long recovery period was hard, restive, and painful. It transformed Samar. The recovery period of his physical healing coincided with a cathartic healing of his mind from the pain of losing Abha and his failure in the exam. He was not sure whether losing Abha was for good or bad, but gradually, he accepted it as God's will. It was a learning experience, a harsh lesson of love and loss. Similarly, the failures, misfortunes, and adverse circumstances encountered so far in the civil services exam were harsh lessons in life. But he was not ready to give up and was determined not to abandon his aspirations at any cost. The frustrations, failures, dejections, heartbreaks, and taunts strengthened his resolve to succeed. Gradually, Abha and her memories faded, replaced by his IAS dreams. Strangely, he missed Old Rajendra Nagar and its alleys, as if he had left an unfinished task. So, in the last week of December 2002, he boarded the Brahmaputra Express to Delhi.

Samar returned to the *gulleys* of Old Rajendra Nagar and rented a single room in another block. Vipul referred him to another property dealer, Mishra*ji*, who helped him negotiate the deal with the landlord. The main entrance led to the stairs and to a common living room on the first floor, with two bedrooms, one of which was for Samar. It was smaller compared to the previous accommodation and had a single bed, an old wooden *almirah*, and a study table and chair. The landlord's son occupied the other bedroom. The bathroom was to be shared by them. The landlord lived on the ground floor. Samar was permitted to use the bathroom geyser for an extra 500 per month.

The landlord's son, Akshat, was hardly there during the day. He had completed an MBA at an Australian university and ran an electronics showroom in Karol Bagh. In his limited interaction with Samar, Akshat boasted about his expensive new car and designer clothes. He indulged in regular drinking sessions with his friends in the living room, which disturbed Samar's evening study sessions on a few occasions.

Samar joined a tuition centre in Rajendra Place to teach students of Classes X to XII. The income was enough to cover his rent, food, and preparations for the third attempt scheduled in May 2003. Soon, he reverted to the IAS preparation cycle.

By the third attempt, an aspirant becomes a veteran of the exam and earns respect from new candidates. Samar was no exception, but he avoided too much contact with new aspirants, as he neither had the time nor the inclination to kindle any association with them. Most of the aspirants he was familiar with had either cleared the examination or had failed and left.

One afternoon in February 2003, Samar's landlady informed him that Akshat was getting married in about two months. She wanted to ask whether he would be comfortable sharing the bathroom with the new bride or whether he would like to vacate the room.

"I have no problem if your son and daughter-in-law have no reservations about sharing the bathroom," he said.

"They won't have any issues," she replied.

As he got up to leave the living room, the landlady gave him a wedding card, saying, "This is your invitation card, Beta. You must come. You are family."

Throughout the next two months, the Mittal household bustled with pre-wedding activities. A week before the wedding, Akshat caught Samar on the stairs. He had his designer groom suit in his hands.

"Hey man! This is my designer suit. How do you like it?"

"It's very nice, Akshat Bhaiya."

"Yes, it is. See the gold-plated buttons and the embroidery. Nice, *na*?"

Samar detested meaningless, unproductive interactions with Akshat. In his opinion, Akshat lacked depth and substance.

Ahead of the wedding day, Samar stayed for two days at Vipul's rented apartment to avoid disturbance before the Prelims, which were just three weeks away.

Samar attended the reception at the nearby Siddharth Hotel. It was the first wedding he attended in Delhi.

The day following the wedding reception, Akshat and his bride, Shraddha, left for their honeymoon to Singapore and Thailand. Samar used the period of their absence to concentrate on his revision.

Samar met the new bride, Shraddha, properly once they returned a fortnight later. She was short, slim, and pretty.

One afternoon, around 4 pm, a week after their return, there was a knock at Samar's door. He opened it and was surprised to see Shraddha standing there.

"Hi, Sameer, right?" she flashed a bright smile.

"No, Samar, *Bhabhiji*." Samar looked around for Akshat.

"Nobody is around. Would you care for some coffee?" Shraddha asked.

"No. Please do not bother, Bhabhiji."

"I will not take 'no' for an answer. I could use some company."

"Okay then, thank you."

"Come out into the living room while I make coffee," Shraddha said.

"Won't Akshat Bhaiya mind it?"

"I don't think so. Besides, he is in Noida. My mother-in-law is downstairs taking her nap."

"Okay, Bhabhiji."

"Please call me Shraddha, not Bhabhiji."

"Won't Akshat Bhaiya mind it?"

"I don't know about your Akshat Bhaiya, but I will definitely mind it," Shraddha chuckled.

Samar responded with a nervous smile.

"Very well."

That helped break the ice between them. As they sipped coffee and ate biscuits, Shraddha talked about herself. She had little ambition or career orientation and seemed to look forward to a life of marital bliss.

"So, tell me about yourself," she said after a while. "Do you have a girlfriend?"

"No!" Samar coloured.

"I'm sorry if my question embarrassed you," Shraddha said, amused.

"Nothing like that! Bhabhiji, my full focus is on clearing the civil services exam. I have already failed in two attempts. I don't want any distraction."

"But having a girlfriend need not be a distraction. She can support you," remarked Shraddha.

"Yes, that's true, Bhabhiji."

"Stop calling me Bhabhiji. It makes me feel old," Shraddha grimaced and continued, "Mummy*ji* said you are taking the exam to become an officer and earn loads of money."

"Oh! Honestly, Shraddha Ji, I want to serve my country and people. A civil servant does get a decent salary but not loads of money."

"Mummy*ji* was referring to *uppar ki* income. My distant *mamaji* was a government official. He made a lot of *uppar ka paisa*, bought an expensive car, clothes, and jewellery for *mamiji*."

"Everyone is not the same. I aspire to be a sincere, compassionate, and efficient officer. I will not compromise on my integrity."

"I am sure God will see your sincerity and integrity. Don't worry, you will get selected." Shraddha was impressed.

"I don't know how to showcase my qualities when the entire focus of the exam is on scoring marks in optionals and General Studies. They don't judge our personality enough with just a 300-mark personality test out of the whole selection process," lamented Samar.

"I will pray for your success before Maa Vaishnoji. I am visiting Mataji's shrine the day after tomorrow with Akshat."

"Have a pleasant journey, Shraddha ji."

***

A month after the wedding, Akshat resumed the noisy drinking sessions with his friends. Samar could also overhear dialogues from the latest serials on TV channels from Shraddha's bedroom.

The Prelims were on the coming Sunday. Samar's centre was at the UPSC hall in Dholpur House. He was satisfied with his performance, and was experienced enough to know he would clear the Prelims.

The results were out in the first week of August 2003. As he had expected, Samar cleared the Prelims. Vipul and Udit also made it to the next stage.

Four months had passed since the wedding. The frequency of Akshat's drinking sessions increased. Shraddha confined herself mostly to her room or spent time downstairs in the kitchen. Samar had not encountered her or seen her for a while. Occasionally, he heard loud arguments from their bedroom.

One afternoon, Shraddha knocked on Samar's bedroom door. "I hope I am not disturbing you?" she asked.

She looked in low spirits, her head covered with a *dupatta*. Samar noticed she had lost some weight since he had seen her about two weeks back. He came out into the living room.

"Not at all. I had just come back from my tuition classes and lain down for a bit," he replied.

"I don't know how to say this..." Shraddha said, "I should not discuss internal matters with a stranger... actually, I am very disturbed."

"I don't know what you are trying to say," mumbled Samar.

"I don't know who to talk to. I can't tell my parents."

Samar glanced at the hallway to make sure no one was listening.

"Don't worry about them. They have all gone out to some relative's function for a few hours," she said despondently.

"I heard some loud voices lately, Shraddhaji."

"Yes, you must have heard our arguments. They are demanding dowry. Akshat plans to expand his electronics dealership."

"Oh! It's so disappointing to hear such things."

"During our honeymoon, Akshat told me about his plans to open a new showroom in Paharganj and that he needed funds. It did not occur to me that he would ask my family for funds. For about a fortnight now, he has been insisting I get 25 lakh rupees from my parents," Shraddha said, "My father has a small gas agency. We do not have so much money..."

Tears rolled down her cheeks.

"When they came to finalize the marriage, my father had specifically mentioned that we do not support dowry. He had asked if they had any such demands. My mother-in-law had said they had no expectations or demands. They only wanted a daughter..."

Samar was appalled.

"Actually, she is a manipulative, conniving woman. She keeps poking Akshat to pressurize me."

"I would have never consented to the marriage if I knew the reality," regretted Shraddha, looking down.

She pulled back her *dupatta* to cover her right cheek.

"Have they physically assaulted you, too?" asked Samar.

"Please do not tell them I spoke to you. I am scared," Shraddha said incoherently.

"Shraddha*ji*, trust me. You can tell me."

"He has slapped me on two occasions after the arguments," Shraddha mumbled.

"Oh, my God! That's not acceptable! You must discuss the matter with your parents," Samar advised.

"I can't… I can't tell my father. He will be heartbroken. He had bypass surgery last year. I can't give them tension…" Shraddha sobbed.

The sounds of footsteps came from downstairs.

"I guess they have returned."

Shraddha rushed back to her bedroom.

Akshat looked puzzled to see Samar in the living room. He grinned and asked, "What's up, studious boy? When will you become an officer?"

Without waiting for a reply, he disappeared into his room. He looked heavily drunk. Samar slowly walked back to his room, thinking about the situation. He was glad not to hear any fresh argument that night.

***

"Who is the hot lady I saw while coming upstairs?" Sunny asked.

"Your preference for women seems to have changed. You found the sixty-year-old landlady hot?" Samar teased.

"Very funny. I meant the young one. She seemed newly wedded."

"Oh yes, Shraddha, Akshat's wife."

"Okay. But why are you blushing?" Sunny teased him.

"So, now it's your turn to pull my leg. She is a married woman. She is a bit disturbed these days."

"You must have rejected her advances!"

"Shut up! Be serious sometimes."

"Okay. First, finish your beer like this." Sunny gulped the remaining beer in his bottle at one go. They were sitting and talking in Samar's room.

"You know me. I drink slowly. I am not as fast as you, whether in drinking or in life."

"*Hahahaha!* I know. You are a turtle in drinking and loving! So, why is such a pretty lady disturbed?" asked Sunny.

"They are demanding dowry from her family."

"Oh! That's terrible! Such a pretty girl is not enough for them. This Akshat fellow must be a jerk!" Sunny said.

"Yes. He is obsessed with money and expensive stuff. He has no depth or morality. A lousy fellow," Samar replied.

"She should seek help from the police. I can help if needed."

"I told her to lodge a complaint, but she is hesitant."

"Why?"

"Social pressure. She does not want to trouble her parents. She hopes things will improve. Anyway, what about you? Are you planning another attempt for the IAS?"

"I am happy with the IPS. I'm not interested in slogging anymore."

"Are you getting AGMUT as you speculated last time?"

"Yes, AGMUT cadre. It's a good cadre for the Police. The commissionerate system is good for IPS. It is there in Delhi, etc."

"And have you found anyone special?" Samar prodded.

"No. You know me! I only like to flirt. No serious business," Sunny answered.

"I don't believe you. You are hiding something… *Chalo*! If you don't want to tell me, it's okay."

"Oh! Don't get touchy! I sort of like this girl from Pune. She got IRS. She is affable and cute. We are good friends, but I don't know if she feels anything for me."

"Oh! So Sunny, the flirt, is finally in love!"

"Just keep it to yourself till something concrete happens."

"Yes, Boss!"

Sunny's IPS training at Sardar Vallabhbhai Pant National Police Academy (SVPNPA) was over. District training was to commence, and Sunny was in transit, so he caught up with Samar and stayed overnight at his place. Sunny's visit thoroughly recharged Samar, and hearing stories about LBSNAA and SVPNPA inspired him further.

***

CHAPTER 11

About a week after Sunny left, Samar saw Shraddha sitting in the living room when he returned from his tuition classes.

Shraddha looked as if she was on the brink of a breakdown.

"You don't look fine, Shraddha..."

"I am depressed. Akshat demanded that I ask for 10 lakhs from my parents. When I said I can't, he got enraged..."

She lifted the sleeve of her *kurta* to expose a bluish-black hematoma on her outer left arm above the elbow. Samar was infuriated.

"This is not done! You must speak to your parents."

"I can't burden them with my problems."

"What are you saying? You are an educated person. It is wrong to endure such torture."

"It is my fate now." Tears trickled down her cheeks.

"Demanding dowry is illegal. You need to file a complaint with the police immediately," Samar advised.

"Let me think it over. I will plead with Akshat... maybe he will understand."

"If you behave like this, he will get more aggressive. You should approach the police. I have an IPS friend. Let me ask him what to do."

"I don't want to make a hasty decision. My family's reputation is involved, and my two younger sisters are yet to be married," said Shraddha. "Your exams are around the corner. I don't want you to get distracted with my problems."

"Don't worry about my exams. Take a wise decision, Shraddha."

Samar had started addressing her as Shraddha in private.

"Thank you so much for listening to me, Samar. I feel better."

"Anytime!"

"I like talking to you. You have dreams and aspirations, some goals to achieve, to look ahead in life..."

***

The Mains exams were fast approaching. Samar procured

the latest notes on Current Affairs taught in Rajan's and other prominent IAS coaching circles from the popular bookshop that thrived on UPSC aspirants. He studied alone this time. Two shots at the UPSC were enough to know what to focus on.

Occasionally, his mind diverted to Shraddha's ordeals whenever he overheard their arguments. He felt the urge to confront Akshat. However, he controlled himself for the sake of the impending exams. He wanted to avoid any trouble which might affect his attempt. He repented the lost chance in his second attempt.

The day before his first paper, he found a card slipped through the bedroom door. The message was sweet:

All the best for the exams, my friend. May Mata Rani bestow her blessings on you to achieve your goals.

Best wishes,

Shraddha.

P.S.: *I am going to my parents for a fortnight. I will try to talk to them about the dowry demand and try to find a solution. Thank you for your advice.*

Samar was glad that Shraddha had gone to her parents. The fortnight passed peacefully in the house. Akshat did not host any party at home. Perhaps the landlady told him about Samar's exams. Akshat was mostly out, partying with his friends.

Samar had a mixed attempt at GS. He struggled to finish GS Paper II on time. The optional papers were better. The essay topics were unexpected, causing him some apprehension. Overall, it was a decent attempt, far better than his previous Mains attempt.

After the examinations, as usual, the aspirants waited for the next phase with hopes of crossing the second barrier of the three-stage examination, aptly called 'the mother of all examinations' in India.

***

Shraddha was back after a fortnight. She appeared visibly relaxed, perhaps because of her stay at her parents' house.

"I am pretty sure you have done well," she said to Samar.

"Not really. I am stressed. Perhaps, it will be my last shot at it. If I don't clear it, I might have to return to Assam."

"Don't think negatively. I am sure you will sail through. Here, have this *prasad*."

She had visited the *Vaishno Devi* shrine with her parents.

"I felt peaceful after the visit. *Mata Rani* is very kind and will help us. *Mata Rani* will guide and protect you. Have faith," Shraddha said.

"Did you talk to your parents?"

"Well… I…" hesitated Shraddha. "I told them. My father was in a state of shock. He did not know what to do or say. We visited *Mata Vaishno Devi* for peace and solace. Now I feel strong enough to face Akshat and my in-laws."

"And how will you face them?" Samar asked her.

"I don't know. I will fight through… maybe it is my destiny. Who can change one's destiny?" Shraddha rested her forehead on her palms, looking unsure and unsettled.

"Shraddha, you cannot accept it as your destiny. Don't let them crush your self-esteem and dignity."

Shraddha avoided his gaze as she tried to divert the discussion. "Hmm… Let's drop the topic. I feel exhausted discussing and thinking about it all the time."

"Avoiding it won't make it go away."

"What happens next if you clear the Mains?"

"Okay, as you say. If I clear the Mains phase, I have to face the interview."

"I have a hunch you are going to clear it this time. Gear up for the next phase, Mr Officer!"

***

Winter was back. Samar embarked on a solo trip to Rishikesh. He chose an ashram in Rishikesh where one could stay, practise yoga with other inmates, eat, and sleep peacefully. Samar deserved a break after toiling for the last nine to ten months. Repeated revisions, fear of failure, and anxiety about the future and Shraddha, overwhelmed his mind. The trip refreshed his mind, body, and soul. Yoga and interactions with yogis were cathartic.

A week after his trip, he heard a loud row at the Mittals'. It was an all-out, loud fight. In the couple's bedroom, the landlady, her husband, and Akshat were arguing and abusing Shraddha, one by one.

"You don't understand the situation. You know how much Akshat needs funds for his expansion," the landlady said. "We have been so patient with you and your family."

"When you went to your home, I thought you had gone to arrange at least 10 lakhs. What did you do there? Just cry and complain?" mocked the landlady.

"Mummy*ji*, we don't have that kind of money," Shraddha pleaded.

"Then ask your father to take a loan. We can refer him to some moneylenders."

"He has limited income, Mummy*ji*," Shraddha tried to reason.

The landlady lost patience with her. She shouted, *"Banti toh tum aise ho jaise kahin ki princess ho! Phir tum sab itne bhikhari kyon ho?"* (You pretend to be a princess! Then why is your family like beggars?)

"Kangle log hain yeh! Humne socha tha gas agency hain, paise hongey. Yeh toh kangle nikle!" (They are broke. We thought they had a gas agency, so they would have money. They have turned out to be broke.)

"Arre yeh sab iska drama hain. Haraamzaadi kahin ki!" abused Akshat. (All this is her drama. She is a bitch!)

"Jab aap log rishta le ke aaye the, tab papa ne pucha tha koi demand toh nahin hain. Aisa hota to hum aage hi nahin badhte!" Shraddha replied. (When you all came with the marriage proposal, then my father had clearly asked if you had any demands. If we had known this, we would not have moved forward with this marriage.)

"Kitni haazir jawaab hai yeh. Yeh aise nahin maanegi. Isko sabak seekhana hoga!" declared the landlady. (How promptly she replies! She will not listen to us like this. She needs to be taught a lesson!)

Samar heard Shraddha pleading and shrieking, "*Nahin*! *Nahin*! Please!" (No! No! Please!)

"Dekh kya raha hain, Akshat, bata isko jawaab dene ka natija!" (What are you looking at, Akshat? Show her the consequences of talking back to us.)

"Nahin! Bhagwan ke liye! chhod do mujhe!" (No! Please leave me for God's sake!)

"Aaahhh..... aahhh...uhh... Hey Mata Rani!... Nahin..."

Samar heard Shraddha shrieking in pain, pleading with them. They gagged her to silence her shrieks. Shocked and enraged, he had a powerful urge to barge into the room. His mind cautioned him not to react impulsively, as it might deteriorate the situation further. He wanted to help, but by using some legal means.

After 10 minutes, he heard footsteps coming out of the room and retreating downstairs. Akshat and the landlady seemed to have left the room. Muffled wails replaced Shraddha's initial shrieks. Samar continued to hear her wails for a while, until an uneasy calm descended upon the house. The physical violence and mental trauma suffered by Shraddha haunted his conscience all night.

The next morning, Shraddha spent the entire day in her room. The maid brought her food, but she refused to eat. She was shocked by the extent of mistreatment meted out by her husband, encouraged by her mother-in-law, a woman herself.

Samar checked on Shraddha when nobody was around. She had swollen eyes from weeping through the night. Samar demanded to see any marks on her. She showed a swollen arm that had been twisted forcefully. Her upper arm had dark brownish burn marks.

"He put a hot iron on my arm..." Shraddha whimpered.

"Horrendous! He is a monster... Bastard!" Samar shouted.

"I am broken from inside... emotionally drained... How can he stoop so low?"

"Only a monster can do such things. You should seek action!" Samar was incensed.

"I am helpless. It is my destiny," Shraddha started weeping. He patted her head.

"You can't tolerate all this. You must file a police complaint immediately," Samar reasoned.

Shraddha lifted her head and lamented, "What alternative do I have? I have two younger sisters. If my marriage breaks up, it will affect their future marriage prospects. I am in a hopeless situation..."

"Don't lose hope. Lodge a complaint with the police. I will accompany you to the police station," Samar said. "If you do not do anything, I will lodge a complaint."

Shraddha looked alarmed. She took his hands and said, "No… No… I will speak to them. Please do not get involved. I don't want any trouble for you, Samar."

It was time for Samar to leave for his tuition. He told her to come to him whenever she wanted.

Samar decided to approach the local police and lodge a complaint. Late afternoon, he reached Rajendra Nagar Police Station.

"Sir, I came to report a crime," Samar said.

The police constable at the desk eyed him with suspicion. He was a middle-aged *paan*-chewing fellow with a paunch.

"What is the matter?" the constable asked.

"I am a tenant at 20/12, Old Rajendra Nagar. The landlords and their son, Akshat, are harassing their daughter-in-law, Shraddha, for dowry," Samar reported.

"Oh, I see!" The constable paused and looked at Samar from head to toe. "How are you connected? Why are you getting involved in their private matter?"

"The daughter-in-law is hesitant to report the matter. So, I am doing it… Sir, it is for you to take action."

"Are you a reporter?" the constable retorted.

"No, Sir, I am an IAS aspirant. I want to lodge a complaint as a vigilant citizen."

"Oh ho! Aping Amitabh Bachchan! Angry young man of Rajendra Nagar! Why don't you concentrate on your own studies?" The constable chuckled.

"Sir, it is not right. You need to take action."

"I will take action as deemed fit. Now, I suggest you go home."

"Sir, what action will you take? Please register a complaint. Please, Sir, help her. She is suffering." Samar folded his hands.

"The police will take appropriate action. You wait and watch. Now, allow me to attend to others, please."

"Can I meet the SHO also?"

"Why? You don't trust me? He is not here," grumbled the constable.

Samar turned to leave. He heard the constable curse behind his back. Samar wasn't sure that the constable would take action, but he had no choice.

***

"Open the door, you bastard!"

There was a loud banging on Samar's bedroom door. He glanced at his wrist watch. It was around 8 pm.

"Open up. Are you scared already?"

Samar was caught off guard as he opened the door. Akshat barged in furiously and caught his shirt collar. With bloodshot eyes, Akshat shouted, "You bastard! How dare you?"

"Let go of my collar," Samar demanded.

"How dare you interfere in my life? Who do you think you are?"

Samar caught hold of Akshat's hands at his collar to break free. The scuffle lasted for a few seconds, after which Samar managed to free himself.

Hearing the commotion, Shraddha came rushing in. Akshat raised his fist to punch Samar. Samar ducked, and Akshat missed him barely. Samar caught hold of Akshat's arms and asked, "What do you want? What is the matter?"

"What is the matter? Don't try to act smart with me!"

Shraddha caught Akshat from behind, trying to pull him away.

"Akshat, please do not do this! Calm down!" she shouted.

"Don't get into this, Shraddha!" He pushed her aside.

Akshat caught hold of Samar's shoulders and shouted, "Why did you go to the police?"

"Why did you hit Shraddha?"

"How dare you take my wife's name? How is it your business?"

Shraddha pleaded, "Please stop all this."

In a fit of renewed rage, Akshat pushed Samar forcefully. Samar fell backwards, hitting his head hard on the side of the bed, almost causing him to lose consciousness.

"Samar! Samar! Are you alright? What have you done, Akshat?" Shraddha shouted.

"Shut up, you whore! The bastard deserves it. I will break all his bones." Akshat was in a fit of uncontrolled rage.

Meanwhile, hearing the commotion upstairs, the senior Mittals rushed in.

Samar got up shakily.

"Ask this bastard to leave this house immediately," Akshat shouted.

"Calm down, Beta! Let me handle it. Shraddha, take Akshat to your room."

"Mom, he tried to lodge a complaint with the police."

"I know, Beta. Let me handle it."

She forced Akshat to leave the room with Shraddha.

Turning her attention to Samar, the landlady said, "Beta, it is really unfortunate what you did. I thought you wanted to become a big officer…"

"Auntie, do not preach to me. I know how you all have been mistreating Shraddha."

"Shraddha is lying! Nothing but melodrama! Leave it! You should vacate the room by tomorrow evening," she commanded.

The landlady left Samar's room. Akshat kept shouting curse words for a while in his room while Shraddha tried to pacify him.

Things calmed down after about half an hour. Disgusted and enraged, Samar left the house. He wandered aimlessly for a while on the streets before deciding to meet Vipul. Vipul agreed with what Samar had done. He reasoned, "You did your best, Samar. But it is Shraddha's call. She needs to decide."

"But she is not going to take any action. It is not right."

"Samar, you must realize that you cannot intervene more than you already did. Besides, don't invite any more trouble for yourself. This is a crucial time for you."

"Maybe you are right. Anyway, they have asked me to vacate. I need to find another room through Mishra*ji*."

"Anoop has vacated his room next to me. You can approach Mishra Ji. You are also welcome to stay in my room if you are comfortable."

"No... No! I will manage. I am going to meet Mishra Ji tomorrow."

***

"Arre, bhool jayeeye aise chhoti chhoti baaton ko, Samar Ji. Aap toh bahut badhe officer banne jaa rahe ho," Mishra Ji said. ("Forget such small incidents, Samar Ji. You are going to be a big officer.")

"But according to the deal, they need to give me one month's notice to vacate the room."

"Arre, Samarji, aisa nahin hota. Yeh sub kehne ki baaten hain. Aap bhi wahaan ek aur mahina kaise rahenge, itna kuch hone ke baad. Main aapko aur acche deals doonga. Abhi thoda manda hain business," Mishra Ji replied. (Samar Ji, it's not like that. All this is just said. How will you stay there for a month after so much has happened? I will get you better deals in some time. Business is a going a bit slow right now.)

Samar shifted to Vipul's floor. Samar had paid one month's rent as an advance to the Mittals. They returned the advance through Mishra Ji.

The unpleasant events at the Mittals made Samar reclusive and pensive for about a fortnight. He felt restless when he thought about what Shraddha might be enduring helplessly, knowing he had no control over the situation. His resolve to clear the exam received another boost—if he were an officer, he could have legally intervened and had the Mittals arrested. As an aspirant, he had complained at the police station, but it backfired. The local constable was known to the Mittals. Instead of taking any cognizance of the matter, he settled for a bottle of whiskey to ignore the complaint. The SHO shut his mouth for half a lakh.

The new accommodation was a small room without a window. It got pitch dark in the night as if it was made to be 'light-proof'. The smutty walls cried for a coat of paint, which Mishra*ji* had promised, but like a seasoned property dealer, his words were hollow. Samar gave up on the idea of a paint job and waited for the Mains results to be declared.

If I clear the exam, I will leave the floor; if I fail, I might have to leave Delhi for good.

***

CHAPTER 12

UPSC declared the Mains results in the first week of March 2004, and to his relief, Samar qualified for the personality test, popularly known as an interview. Among his acquaintances, Udit qualified, but Vipul failed.

The IAS coaching circles around Rajendra Nagar were abuzz with activities, offering coaching for the interview. Samar put his faith in Rajan's again and joined it. The interview preparation was different from the usual Prelims and Mains stages. The major thrust of the personal test/interview would be on personality assessment, analytical ability, situational alertness, and the smartness of the candidate, and not just knowledge-testing. The coaching classes devoted sessions to what to expect, how to answer tricky questions, body language, appearance, mannerisms, and etiquette. Much emphasis was given to seemingly small things, such as how to enter the room, greet and exchange pleasantries with the interview board:

"Always wish the chairperson first and then the board members."

"Wish the lady member separately, if any lady member is on the board."

"Always maintain eye contact with all the members."

"Always wear a benign, pleasing smile."

"Always answer courteously and confidently. If you show an iota of nervousness, it will definitely go against you."

"At the end, say, 'Have a nice day, Sirs and Madams!'"

In the hobbies section, Samar had jotted down his hobbies as reading fiction and writing. According to the coaching circle experts, Samar's hobbies were common and stereotypical, and probably the board would ignore them.

The coaching centre organized group discussion sessions on trending current affairs or political issues. They stressed that whatever one's affiliation—rightist, leftist, or centrist—one should not expose it. Instead, one should only project balanced, unbiased views. Responses should project the aspirant as a broad-minded, balanced, upright, and pragmatic individual.

The coaching circle invited a few successful candidates to give valuable tips. Such sessions were quite popular among the aspirants, who posed all sorts of questions.

Mock interviews were conducted towards the end of the coaching sessions. Samar attended a couple of mock interviews and feedback sessions for practice. He took the feedback seriously and worked on himself. He made a list of the likely questions that may be posed to him—about Bangladeshi infiltration, the Assam students' movement, the Assam agitation, the demand for Bodoland, etc.

***

Samar dressed for the personality test in a new, crisp, sky-blue formal shirt, navy-blue pleated trousers, a navy-blue plain tie, polished black shoes, and a newly purchased Titan watch. Samar's test was on the 'first day, first show' of the UPSC Personality Test schedule. It was a bright, sunny day. He was glad that the interview was at a relatively cooler time of the day, as it might become difficult to maintain a crisp and sweat-free shirt during the scorching summer afternoon of April.

A pre-booked taxi dropped him at Dholpur House at 9:00 am sharp. The Dholpur House complex was like a citadel. One had to be privileged and important enough to enter the perimeter. Samar was one of the 900-odd aspirants who had made it to the personality test stage. A few street vendors had lined up their food carts along the side lane near the entry gate. They were experienced vendors who knew they could make brisk business over the next 25 days or so, until the UPSC aspirants kept coming to Dholpur House.

The entry at the gate was smooth. Directions at a few points led to a circular room with a dome. Samar was one of the earliest to arrive.

So, this is the room where, year after year, aspirants wait for their turn to face the board.

Udit was sitting in a corner, wearing a light pink shirt, dark brown trousers, and a brown tie. Samar greeted him. Udit merely said "Hi" and looked away. Anxiety was written all over his face!

Samar settled into one of the vacant chairs, away from Udit, to avoid any negativity on such an important day. He noticed several round tables with chairs around them placed in the hall. They had cardboards, each displaying a number from one to six.

"They are numbered corresponding to the number of interview boards today," a thin fellow, seated a few chairs away, explained.

"Oh! I see. How do you know?" Samar smiled.

"Trust me, I know. This is my fifth interview! I hope I don't face a 'stress interview' this time," he chuckled nervously.

He introduced himself as Yudhvir Yadav. He told Samar that candidates will sit around the tables assigned to them by the board. Gradually, more and more candidates arrived in the hall. All were dressed in formal shirts and trousers or crisply starched cotton sarees. They were 18 in total. Some were cheerful and chatty, while a few were quiet. Some looked serious, while a few looked nervous. Udit did not interact with anyone. He had visited the restroom twice since his arrival.

An official came and announced the table number where the candidates were supposed to sit. Samar was allotted table number one with two other candidates, both ladies. The official checked the certificates and testimonials of the aspirants. The two ladies at Samar's table were Priyanka Mishra and P. Sara Joseph. Both of them were on their first attempt.

P. Sara Joseph was the first candidate to be interviewed by Board no. 1. A peon courteously escorted her away. After another 20 minutes, he returned to escort Samar. The interview room was about 40 or 50 metres away. The peon gestured to him to sit in an empty chair just outside the room. He felt his legs shaking a bit and his heartbeat thumping loudly as he waited. He silently recited prayers to Lord Krishna. After 10 minutes, P. Sara Joseph came out of the room with a broad smile. She wished him luck in a low tone as she walked away confidently. Samar smiled nervously.

After another silent prayer, Samar stood and entered the interview room. The door was thick, solid wood, unwieldy and heavy, and required a push to open. Samar pushed hard at the door, entered, and shut it behind him. He tried to make eye contact with the chairman at the outset, but he was busy reading something on his desk. The door made a little more noise than it should have. Samar seemed to have pushed it back harder than required.

That was bad!

The chairman was startled by the noise and looked up. A cold, electric impulse ran through Samar's body.

"That was quite an entry, young man!" he said, as two other members chuckled, while another looked annoyed.

Samar greeted the board members quickly with a faint smile. There was no lady member present. There were five members, including the chairman, with a nameplate inscribed Alok Kumar Agarwal. The names of the members were inscribed on the nameplates placed in front of them, but Samar did not dare to stare long. He sat down as soon as the chairman said, "Please sit down."

"Mr Samar, can you tell us how you are different from any other candidate?" the chairman asked.

The question puzzled Samar. He had neither expected such a question nor had an answer practised for it. He knew he had to answer quickly.

"Sir, I am not different from any other aspirant. Every aspirant comes with a definite goal, zeal, and a motto. An aspirant comes to serve the citizens and make a difference for his fellow countrymen through fresh ideas…"

He was interrupted by the chairman, "Pardon me for interrupting, but if every aspirant comes with the same goals, how do we choose from amongst them? What is special about you, Mr Samar Sharma… I mean, Mr Samar Sarma?"

Samar did not want to sound nervous, but he did not have a ready answer.

"Sir, I am not special. I am ordinary, like any other citizen. And I want to work for other ordinary citizens of India. I want to make their lives easier," Samar stopped as he did not want to sound cliché.

"Mr Samar, can't you make the lives of citizens easier from outside the civil services? Why do you presume you can do so only after becoming a civil servant?" the chairman volleyed another unfamiliar question.

"Sir, as a civil servant, I will be able to touch the lives of several citizens. I will have the power and responsibility to implement schemes, draft policies, frame rules and regulations, innovate, and apply new ideas to a larger section of the populace. Outside the civil services, I may not have the authority or the position to do so. Sir, I mean, I will have a wider canvas to work on through the civil services."

"Very well." The chairman gestured to the member seated on his right to carry on. Samar identified him as the one with the annoyed look at his entry.

"Taking further the question asked by Mr Chairman, do you mean that only civil servants can serve the country and others cannot?" he asked.

"Sir, I do not mean to say that only civil servants can serve. Every person can contribute to society, the welfare of fellow citizens, and the country. However, every person chooses their own way to contribute. And my chosen way is through the ambit of the civil services."

"Fair enough. Have you ever faced a situation where you felt, 'I wish I were in a position of power to change this situation?'"

"Yes, Sir. Recently, as a tenant, I witnessed the daughter-in-law of my landlords being subjected to mental and physical harassment by her in-laws for dowry. She was hesitant to report the atrocities. Therefore, as a conscientious citizen, I reported the matter to the local police. However, they did not take any action. Instead, they ignored my complaint and did not even register the case. If I had been an ACP or a District Magistrate, I could have taken cognizance of the matter and taken it to a logical conclusion."

"Fair enough."

He glanced at the chairman, probably to signal that he was through with his questions. The chairman urged the next person to carry it forward. About 15 minutes had passed.

"Mr Samar, as you belong to Assam, I am sure you are well aware of the Bangladeshi infiltration across the border. What are the causes of such infiltration?"

Aah! It's a tricky question, but an expected one. Answer it cautiously and diplomatically!

"Sir, we need to understand the root causes for the infiltration. Factors like poverty and inequality compel people to migrate, leaving behind their native places, in search of a livelihood and a better life."

"What solution can you suggest to discourage the infiltrators?"

"Sir, we should try to provide such people access to resources and a livelihood in their native places. That will discourage infiltration."

Next, the gentleman who had chuckled at Samar's entry turned to him.

"Mr Sarma, what is the ST population in the Northeast?"

"Sir, I am afraid I do not remember the total figure."

"I am surprised, Mr Sarma, you do not remember that when you hail from the Northeast. Anyhow, Assam is a predominantly rural state. Can you tell me what the percentage of the rural population in Assam is?"

"Yes, Sir. If I remember correctly, it is around 85 per cent."

"Mr Sarma, since over $3/4^{th}$ of Assam's population lives in rural areas, naturally, the state's development will be linked to that of the rural areas. Can you suggest what can be done for their development?"

"Sir, Assam has vast potential in rural areas in sectors like fish farming in local ponds and lakes; horticulture; and handloom and cottage industries like *Muga* and *Eri* silkworm rearing, where predominantly women are involved. Such sectors need to be encouraged through investment, hand-holding, self-help groups, and market access for their products."

The last gentleman turned to Samar. "It's good to hear your ideas. Do you agree that the centre has neglected the Northeast?"

"Sir, I don't think so. However, there is less awareness about the Northeast among the rest of the population of India."

"Can you elaborate further, Mr Samar?"

"Sir, starting from our history books, there is hardly any mention of the kingdoms and dynasties that existed in the Northeast vis-à-vis the rest of India. The culture, customs, traditions, cuisine, and rituals of the Northeast are different, but people do not have exposure to the culture of the region as a whole."

Finally, the chairman reclaimed the interview.

"You have written that reading is your hobby. What do you read?"

"Sir, mainly classics."

"Do you have any favourite books?"

"*Wuthering Heights*, Sir."

"Very well, Mr Samar. It was good to interact with you. Thank you."

Samar thanked every member of the board and walked to the door, carefully closing it behind him. His interview had lasted for about 35 minutes.

Samar walked to the hall to collect his folder. Yudhvir asked him how he had done in his interview.

"Not that great. I am not sure how I will fare in their assessment."

"Okay. Hope to see you again."

Samar waved at him and slowly made his way out of the complex. This might be his last entry in the elusive Dholpur House.

***

About two months later, in the first week of May 2004, Vipul rushed into Samar's room to inform him that the CSE final results were out. A cold shiver ran through Samar.

Will I make it? Will I find my name on the list? I have not even considered alternative career options.

Samar and Vipul took an auto to the UPSC. The ride felt long, arduous, and stressful.

A small crowd had gathered at the UPSC notice board as anxious aspirants and their well-wishers jostled one another, trying to scan the list. Some aspirants were shouting loudly, congratulating one another, hugging, or patting each other excitedly, while others who could not find their names on the list quietly withdrew from the scene, dejected.

Samar could feel his heart thumping hard as he scanned the list. He could not find his name. He rechecked the list hurriedly, but could not find his name again. In the last three years, Samar had encountered several failures. He had failed twice, fallen in love with Abha but lost her, lost his budding friendship with Shraddha, and lost his share in his ancestral property. Feeling weak, he dragged himself to the stairs and sat down. He felt a lump in his throat and an ache in his heart…

How will I face society, Amar da, Maloti bau, relatives, and friends?

The future looked bleak…

***

"Get up, you idiot!"

Vipul had scanned the list a second time and had come running up to Samar. He tried to pull him up.

"You have cleared. You made it!" Vipul yelled, thumping Samar's shoulder.

Samar found his words hard to believe. With Vipul's help, he got up and walked to the notice board to check the list again.

He found his name this time.

Vipul said loudly, "I told you. You have made it, Samar!"

Other aspirants standing at the board looked at Samar with respect. In a few moments, it was as if the whole world had changed.

Vipul hugged him. Unknown aspirants congratulated him.

It took a while for the feeling to sink in….

The trials of the last three years flashed before his eyes. More than anything else, Samar felt relieved and vindicated.

Samar's brother and nephew were overwhelmed with joy on hearing the news. His sister-in-law remarked, "I always knew you would make it." He smiled wryly, finding it ironic.

Udit failed to qualify and left for Mumbai for good.

***

For the next few days, Samar was happy and relaxed. He could sleep peacefully at night. However, clearing the 'mother of all exams' didn't feel as euphoric as he had imagined it would be. It was probably because the exam was a long process, marked by long waits and failures, and painful experiences.

Nevertheless, Samar became a sought-after person among fresh aspirants who flocked to him for tips on studying.

Samar visited Guwahati 10 days after the final results. Relatives and neighbours visited, and congratulated him. Everyone became sweet and respectful.

"We always knew you would make it."

"You are a role model for others in our family."

"Can you guide my son on how to prepare for the exam?"

He returned to Delhi and visited the *Vaishno Devi* shrine to pay his respects. The last time he had visited, he had made a promise to walk barefoot up to the shrine if the *Devi* fulfilled his dream. He kept his promise.

Samar received a letter from the UPSC, informing him that he had been allotted DANICS, one of the many services for which the UPSC conducts the common CSE. Samar had filled DANICS, also known as the Union Territory Civil Services (UTCS) cadre, as his ninth choice among the services. His rank was 332. The total number of candidates recommended was 413.

The training for DANICS was to commence at the beginning of 2005. Samar continued the tuition classes to cover his living expenses in Delhi.

Abha would have been very happy at his success. He wished he could inform her. If only the Zirakpur incident had not happened… if only things had not turned out as they did… if only he had control over the situation then…

He had no information about her, but he assumed she must have gotten married.

***

CHAPTER 13

Samar received a letter from the UPSC stating that training for the DANICS 2004 batch will commence on March 1, 2005, at the UTCS institute in Delhi. On the appointed day, Samar met his batchmates outside the Director's office. The batch was small with just two more batchmates, Naeem Ahmed and Senthil Kumar. Naeem was a B.Tech from Lucknow, and Senthil Kumar had a Master's in Agriculture from Madurai. It was Naeem's second attempt and Senthil's fourth one. Both planned to retake the Civil Services Examination. But Samar was undecided. He had only one attempt left, and it was not financially feasible to spend another year preparing for the exam. There was also no guarantee he would clear the exam again.

It was mandatory for the probationers to remain on campus. The UTCS campus was not what Samar had expected. He had seen photos of LBSNAA, Mussoorie, clicked by Sunny during his foundation phase. The UTCS was not even its poor cousin!

The probation period lasted two years. Training during the first year was essentially classroom-based. Classes were held on various Acts and laws, delivered by guest lecturers ranging from retired or in-service bureaucrats and academicians to practising lawyers, consultants, and public speakers. Some of the prominent Acts covered included the Indian Penal Code (IPC), the CPC, the CrPC, the Delhi Land Reforms Act, and the Delhi Land Revenue Act, as well as their associated rules. Soft skill sessions on time management, project management, stress management, public speaking, and case studies were also conducted. The classes were held from 10 am to 5 pm with a one-hour lunch break. Lunch was served in the officers' mess.

The centre had recreational facilities like an indoor games hall and a badminton court, as well as a library. Compulsory swimming and driving classes were part of the curriculum. The probationers had to clear the swimming and driving tests at the end of the training. Amidst these activities, the first year of training passed.

Training in the second year was practical, with on-field exposure to various departments in Delhi, UT *Darshan*, trekking, and a one-month exposure in another state, district, etc. A few experience-sharing sessions were also conducted in which retired or in-service bureaucrats were invited to interact with the probationers and share their experiences. Samar enjoyed these sessions and also trekking in *Devbhumi*, Uttaranchal. Towards the end of the second year, the UT *Darshan* commenced. The week-long stay in the Andaman and Nicobar Islands and another week in Lakshadweep were memorable. The batch interacted with senior bureaucrats posted at these places. The UT Administration treated them very well during the UT *Darshan*. Snorkelling and scuba diving in Lakshadweep, and the forests and historical places of the Andaman and Nicobar Islands, were etched in their memories.

With the UT *Darshan*, the training period came to an end. UTCS conducted examinations at the end of the probation period. Samar was glad that the training period was ending. He had failed to develop a personal rapport with his batchmates as they were engrossed in preparations for their next attempt.

Samar had regular contact with Vipul and Sunny. Sunny was posted to Arunachal Pradesh. Vipul qualified for the Civil Services Exam, 2006, up to the interview stage, but failed to secure a place on the final list. He was gearing up for his last attempt.

Once Samar cleared the exam, relatives, who had hardly been around when he was struggling, started cajoling him to get married. Amar also raised the subject a few times, urging him to settle down. But Samar wanted to wait a little longer.

The MHA issued a transfer order for the batch at the end of February. Naeem Ahmed had been posted to the Andamans, and Senthil Kumar to Lakshadweep. Samar was retained in Delhi. The transfer order shocked his batchmates as both had put in a word at the MHA for a posting in Delhi. Senthil's father was an IPS officer in the Tamil Nadu cadre, while Naeem was from an influential political family in Bihar, but their influence did not work at the MHA.

Samar reported to the Services Department, Delhi Secretariat, GNCT of Delhi. He also made a courtesy call to the Chief Secretary. A fortnight after the MHA orders, Samar got his first posting in the

VAT department. He was posted as an Assistant Commissioner in charge of some wards in the Chandni Chowk area. The office was in *Vyaapar Bhawan* at Indraprastha Estate.

The VAT Commissioner was Mr Rajiv Kumar, a senior IAS officer. There were other senior IAS and DANICS officers as Special Commissioners, Additional Commissioners, and Joint Commissioners based on their seniority.

The initial one or two months were difficult for Samar. He found it hard to understand the procedure to be followed. The two years of training appeared to be a waste of time. He was familiar with the Acts, rules, and regulations taught during the training, but applying them in actual cases was a different task. However, the senior staff was patient and helpful.

Samar rented an apartment in Dwarka. The long commute was tiring. After reaching home in the evening, he usually lay down for an hour. Later, he would read a book. He listened to the news on TV during dinner. He did not have many friends in Delhi. Sunny Singh had been posted in Central Delhi as an ACP and was very busy. They were in regular touch on the phone but met rarely. Samar felt the need for a companion, a life partner. He was now settled financially, and the time was ripe for marriage.

Amar had suggested Maloti's younger sister to him, but Samar turned it down. He had never connected with the girl on the few occasions he had met her. Besides, he assumed she would not be much different from her sister.

***

Dressed in a light-blue, semi-formal, crisp shirt and dark grey trousers, Samar looked decent, educated, and sharp. He was sitting in a cafe at Paan Bazaar, Guwahati, to meet Jyotsna.

Samar was keen to marry a simple and educated girl from Assam. He had no active social circle, so the chance of finding such a girl in Delhi was remote. He created a profile on an Assamese matrimonial site, Assamese Matrimony. He was not very regular on the site, but a particular message from Dr Robin Deka caught his attention one evening. The profile was of Deka-Jyotsna, a girl from Tezpur.

Dr Deka had been looking for a match for his eldest daughter, Jyotsna, for over a year. He had scanned profile after profile religiously. A Government of India officer, an ACS officer, or a doctor—his preferred choices were rare on the site. He came across Samar's profile, which he liked, and dropped him a message. He received a response from Samar after 2 months, and Samar suggested a meeting.

Samar agreed. He took a week's leave to visit Guwahati. He also decided to visit his brother's family, who had shifted to Sonapur after their house was acquired. Dr Deka hired a cab and visited Guwahati, along with his wife and two daughters, Jyotsna and Meghna. They met Samar and, after a while, left him and Jyotsna to interact with each other.

Jyotsna was stunningly beautiful, with a dusky complexion, lissome figure, sharp facial features, medium-length hair, long eyelashes, smiling eyes, a round face, and average height.

Both Samar and Jyotsna were shy and reserved and struggled to speak. After the initial shyness dissipated, Samar told her about his family background, his struggles in life, his initial failures in the UPSC exam, clearing the exam, and his future dreams and aspirations.

"What are your expectations from a partner?" Samar asked.

"He should be nice, caring, humble, dependable…" Jyotsna replied shyly.

"A boring person, you mean?" Samar teased.

"Being so is not boring."

"Do I meet your criteria?" Samar teased, mildly flirting.

Jyotsna blushed and did not answer. Samar was gazing at her, and she squirmed with excitement. She had hardly interacted with boys before. The brief rendezvous with Samar unfurled thousands of dreams and hopes. For her, Samar, with his good looks, settled career, and good mannerisms, was no less than Prince Charming!

Samar, too, was floored by Jyotsna, and he decided to marry her in a single meeting.

***

Amar made further inquiries about Jyotsna's family. Dr Robin Deka was a retired doctor from the Assam Government. His father originally hailed from Tezpur. As Dr Deka was in a transferable job, the family would move wherever he was posted. Finally, when Jyotsna was in the eighth standard, Mrs Deka, Jyotsna, and Meghna settled down in Tezpur.

Known as Jenny at home, Jyotsna completed her schooling and graduation from Tezpur University. She was an academically-oriented student. The Deka sisters had very little exposure to anything and knew hardly any other place besides their town.

Amar visited the Dekas' at Tezpur and finalized the match. The wedding was fixed for December 10, 2007, at Tezpur. It was a middle-class, decent wedding. Amar, Maloti, Abhimanyu, a few relatives, and Sunny Singh were the only participants from the groom's side. Maloti acted more like a guest than a family member. She held a grudge against Samar for rejecting her sister.

The next day, the newlywed couple flew to Delhi. Jyotsna got a tearful send-off at Guwahati Airport.

There were no family members to perform the rituals of welcoming the new bride into the house in Dwarka. Samar had deposited the keys with a friendly neighbour, Mrs Barua.

"A pretty bride! *Saakshaat Lakshmi Avatar!*" Mrs Barua remarked.

Jyotsna blushed.

"Wait a minute. The bride needs to be welcomed auspiciously."

Samar and Jyotsna waited at the threshold. Mrs Barua came out holding a *puja thaali* with a bowl of rice grains, an earthen lamp, and vermillion. Poornima, her daughter, followed. Mrs Barua placed the rice bowl at the threshold of the entrance.

Jyotsna toppled it with her right foot and entered the house.

"Thank you so much, Aunty!"

Jyotsna and Samar bowed down to touch her feet.

"Arrey! No… No... God bless the lovely couple!" Mrs Barua showered blessings.

"Aunty, please sit down," Samar requested.

The living room was minimalistic, with a simple glass-topped wooden coffee table, a simple two-seater wooden sofa, and two single-seater sofas. Jyotsna promptly stepped into the kitchen, found a tray, and placed two glasses of water, and a plate with the *Kaju barfi* they had picked up on the way from the airport. Mrs Barua and Poornima picked up a piece each.

Poornima studied in college and was younger than her brother, Arnab. Arnab was married and settled in the US. Mr Barua was a retired government doctor. Mrs Barua chattered away till Poornima said, "Mummy, I think we should let Samar da and bau rest. They must be exhausted."

"Yes, yes… don't hesitate to ask if you need anything. You will need time to settle down," Mrs Barua left with these words.

Samar took the luggage into the bedroom, which Jyotsna found cosy. A new Godrej wardrobe stood on the right side of the bed, keys dangling from the keyhole. She hastily wiped off the dust that had settled on the headpiece and side tables of the mahogany bed, an item acquired by Samar as part of the wedding preparations.

"Leave aside the dusting. The maid will clean up tomorrow morning," Samar said.

"We can't sleep on a dusty bed," Jyotsna said, and her heart skipped a beat when she uttered the word 'bed'.

"Will Italian food do for tonight?" asked Samar.

Jyotsna nodded.

"Good. I am ordering a large pizza with black olives, jalapenos and paneer as toppings, along with a plate of garlic bread. Do you want anything else?"

"No," Jyotsna replied.

"Okay. I think I will have a bath, meanwhile." Samar disappeared into the bathroom, taking a towel and some clothes.

Jyotsna stepped into the kitchen. It was a mess. The bachelor pad required a thorough clean-up. She rinsed two plates, a few spoons, and a knife and placed the items on a tray for the evening meal. Then she unpacked her bag and arranged her clothes in the wardrobe.

Samar emerged, refreshed after his bath, in crisp new striped pyjamas and a T-shirt. His washed vest and underwear were in his hands.

"Here, give me your clothes. I will hang them for drying," Jyotsna offered.

"No... No... I will hang them myself," he replied. He felt shy about handing over his clothes to her.

"The pizza will arrive soon. You should bathe, too," Samar said from the balcony.

"I think I will bathe after dinner," Jyotsna replied.

The pizza was delivered soon. They enjoyed their dinner, thinking about their life together ahead.

While Samar switched on the TV to watch the news, Jyotsna took a warm shower. She changed into a comfortable nighty, then put a sleeping gown over it. Then, she waited in the bedroom for Samar.

"Everything ready?" Samar asked loudly.

"Yes," she replied nervously.

Samar switched off the TV and walked gingerly into the bedroom. He felt awkward too. Jyotsna sat on the bed, avoiding his eyes.

Samar switched off the light and sat on the right side of the bed. There was an awkward silence in the room. Jyotsna could hear the loud thumping of her heart.

Samar was nervous, too. In the past few months, since they were engaged, they had spoken on the phone once or twice a week.

"Are you tired?" Samar asked.

"No."

"Do you want to go to sleep now?"

"No."

He took her hand and placed it over his heart.

"Can you feel the pounding? It's for you," he whispered.

Putting his arm around her waist, he gently pulled her closer to him. His fingers played with her hair and caressed the nape of her neck. Her body trembled at his touch that kindled a thousand sensations, hitherto unknown to her.

Samar's lips met hers. His kisses became urgent and demanding. He slowly started to slide the nightie off her shoulders. Their eyes met. Jyotsna shivered and pushed him away slightly.

"Any problem?" mumbled Samar.

"I am a bit uncomfortable," Jyotsna whispered.

"Okay. No problem."

They sat side by side on the bed, holding hands. Samar rested his head on her shoulder. They remained like that for a while before going to sleep, still holding hands.

The next morning, Jyotsna was startled awake by the doorbell.

"It must be the maid," Samar said. He had taken a week off from work. Jyotsna tied her gown over the nighty and answered the door.

"*Namaste Madamji*!" the dusky, middle-aged maid greeted her. She went into the kitchen to wash the utensils.

Jyotsna instructed the maid to prepare breakfast while brewing black tea herself. Samar was up by then, and they sat together on the sofa.

"The tea tastes different today," said Samar.

"Oh! Don't you like it?" asked Jyotsna.

"No. It's just that I don't take sugar with my morning tea," Samar smiled.

"Oh! I am sorry. I did not know."

"That's fine. How will you know?" Samar said. "We will get to know each other's habits gradually."

"Yes."

"I have some books in the other room. You can have a look at them since you are fond of reading."

After breakfast, Samar buried his nose in the newspaper. Jyotsna was glad to see many books neatly stacked on a bookshelf. There were many well-known classics in the collection. She picked *Of Human Bondage* by Somerset Maugham and was soon engrossed in it. The maid completed the housework, cooked lunch, and then left.

***

CHAPTER 14

Jyotsna had never imagined she would marry someone who lived outside Assam. Her family, especially her mother, was apprehensive about her life in a big city. But Jyotsna looked forward to new experiences in a new place.

Two days after they arrived from Guwahati, Samar asked, "Do you want to go out?"

"I would love to."

"Good. Let's go to the Raja Garden Mall. I am sure you will like the place."

On their way to the mall, they held hands, inviting fleeting glances from the taxi driver. The taxi dropped them off at the mall after about 40 minutes. The mall was not too crowded, and its central air conditioning, gleaming floors, and brightly lit stores were new to Jyotsna.

"This is a lovely place!" Jyotsna said.

She walked alongside Samar, clasping his arm.

"Yes, it was opened last year. A nice place to spend time," Samar replied.

"I want to confess something," Jyotsna said with a worried look.

"That you have broken a lot of hearts before!" Samar teased.

"No, no…" said Jyotsna.

"That you have a secret lover!" Samar grimaced.

"Come on… be serious."

"Okay, shoot!"

"I don't know how to cook. I can make omelettes, tea, etc., but I am not a good cook. Maa says I am a bland cook," Jyotsna confessed.

"That's fine. I love to cook occasionally. Speaking of food, what would you like to have for dinner?" Samar asked.

"Maybe some South Indian food," Jyotsna said after thinking for a few seconds.

"They have a decent food court and food joints of all kinds on the upper floor," he said as they moved up the escalator.

They stepped into a popular South Indian restaurant and ordered two Paneer *Dosas* and two glasses of buttermilk. They enjoyed their dinner.

Back from the mall that night, they made love, slowly and hesitantly, unfurling unknown emotions.

The next morning, Jyotsna hid the stained bedsheet from the maid and washed it herself.

***

"Can we buy a dining table and some cutlery?" Jyotsna asked.

"Yes, of course! You should take care of domestic matters from now on," Samar replied.

Jyotsna and Samar spent the majority of the week relaxing at home, eating, sleeping, talking, and making love. Jyotsna also spoke to her sister and parents.

"I am falling in love with Delhi," she assured them.

Samar rejoined work after the week was over. Jyotsna spent her time rearranging sofas, side tables, kitchenware, and other items. A four-seater glass-topped dining table, a wooden-and-glass showcase, an OTG, and an automatic washing machine were added to the household within a month. Samar had a preference for certain electronic brands, and Jyotsna gladly agreed to his choices.

They left for their honeymoon to the Andaman Islands two months after their marriage. They visited Havelock, Diglipur, Baratang, Port Blair, and Wandoor. While on honeymoon, Samar received news of his transfer to the Revenue Department as SDM in the Southwest District.

After they returned, Samar joined as SDM Kapashera. Jyotsna, a PhD holder in Plant Genetics, joined as a post-doctoral fellow in the Genetics Department at South Campus, Delhi University, in Professor Rajanna's lab. The work involved molecular analysis of transgenic tomatoes developed in the laboratory by a previous PhD student.

Gradually, they both settled down. Although Jyotsna was happy to resume research, she found the bus ride to South Campus troublesome. Hailing from a small town like Tezpur, she was not accustomed to long commutes on overcrowded buses. Samar urged her to get an auto or a taxi, but she did not want to spend too much of Samar's salary or her limited stipend. She travelled in autos only occasionally.

The mornings on weekdays were rushed. Samar's working hours were long. He reached back home late in the evening. His responsibilities as SDM and the work were far greater than his previous assignment in VAT. Jyotsna also returned around 7 pm.

She occasionally complained about Samar's long working hours. Samar would return, exhausted from the day, as Jyotsna did. She expected him to spend the rest of the evening with her. But Samar spent much of the evening relaxing and watching the news on TV. She did not complain to him. She thought that, as a married man, he should know her expectations. Gradually, she began spending her evenings talking to her family. They both retired to bed early on weekdays.

Weekends were much better, as both had a half-day at work. They occasionally dined out on a Saturday. They spent Sunday talking, sleeping, and lazing around. Jyotsna also read *Of Human Bondage* on weekends. She was more than halfway into the book.

Mrs Barua and Poornima often talked to her on weekends. Jyotsna did not encourage them much, as weekends were the only days to relax, rewind, and spend time with Samar. Mrs Barua was indulgent and intrusive, trying to extract information about her and Samar: "Is everything good?", "Hope Samar is taking good care of you. Let me know if you need anything!", "Samar is like my son, you know!", "Don't hesitate for anything."

Jyotsna felt tempted to snap. "Why would I tell you anything?" I have my parents and sister for that! But she refrained from doing so. After all, Mrs Barua was helpful and kind. Poornima had a boyfriend and liked to blabber about him whenever Mrs Barua was not around.

As the initial euphoria of a new married life fizzled out and mundaneness began to set in, she felt something was missing. She began to compare Samar with her father, how he used to behave and treat her. In this comparison, Samar was beginning to fall short. She also missed the camaraderie and time with her sister. She wondered if life would have been better with Samar in Tezpur.

***

Samar occasionally socialized with Sunny. On such evenings, they would meet after office hours for dinner and drinks, and Samar would come home late. Jyotsna's father was a teetotaller. Before their marriage, she did not know that Samar drank hard liquor. As she had no exposure to the drinking culture in her family, she did not like it.

They had their first fight about three months after their marriage, when he staggered home around 10:30 pm on a weekday.

She opened the door.

"Hey, Wifey. How are you doing?"

She returned to the bedroom without a word.

"What happened, Wifey? Why are you so glum?" Samar asked, following her.

Sitting on the bed silently, Jyotsna fidgeted with the pillow cover, disgusted to see him stagger in.

"Are you upset because I came home late? I just had a few drinks with Sunny. Chill *yaar*!" Samar stood unbuttoning his shirt.

"I think my wife is angry today," Samar made a face,"I had a long day, Wifey. I am exhausted by the travel."

"You are tired? You have a driver! I travel daily in buses, come home to make dinner, and you spend time with your friends," she finally said.

"I have told you several times to take a taxi. But, you don't listen."

"I want to save money, so I travel in buses!"

"Then don't blame it on me!"

"I am just mentioning it, not blaming you! What I don't like is that you prefer spending time with friends more than you like coming home to me. And these friends? Don't they have wives and families waiting at home?" Jyotsna argued.

"I told you in the afternoon that I have plans with Sunny. You should not have waited for me. You did not eat *kya*?" Samar spoke in a soft tone.

"How does it matter to you whether I ate or not? You ate, didn't you? That's sufficient!"

"You shouldn't have waited for me when I told you I have plans, Jenny."

"Why do men drink? My father doesn't drink. Is he not living a life?"

"Everyone is different, Jenny."

"My father is an ideal man. He loves my mother, cares for her and his two girls. I thought you would want to emulate his qualities."

"I don't want to emulate anyone," Samar retorted irritably.

"How can you? You are nowhere near his level! No one in your family is!" Jyotsna yelled.

"Don't compare me with your father or bring my family into this." Samar glared at her, losing his temper.

"Why shouldn't I compare? And what about your family? Do you have one? I saw your brother and Maloti bau. Do they even care for you? They came to the wedding like guests," Jyotsna yelled.

"Just because you have a close family and I don't, you have no right to criticize my family. And don't force me to open my mouth about your *ideal father*," Samar yelled back.

"What did you say about my father?"

"I know about his suspension! So, don't give me that 'my great father' nonsense!" Samar shouted, walking out of the room.

Jyotsna turned red with anger and burst out crying. She had not eaten anything. She missed her family. In frustration, she locked the bedroom door from inside and fell on the bed, whimpering.

Samar was greatly disturbed. He regretted saying those things about her father. He turned on the TV and flicked through channels till late at night. He fell asleep on the sofa in the wee hours of the morning.

It took them three days to come back to speaking terms and another week for things to return to normal.

***

Jyotsna hired a maid specifically to cook breakfast, lunch, and dinner, in addition to the one who did the cleaning. They bought an AC to deal with the blistering summer heat. Jyotsna's mother urged her to plan for a child. But sex was limited to once or twice a week, mostly on the weekend.

Meghna visited them for a month. Jyotsna was glad, as she now had a companion to chat with after a hard day. She noticed Samar spoke less and spent a lot of time reading the newspaper and watching the news. Jyotsna did not read the newspaper or listen to the news much. But she loved to watch tele-serials and movies. Samar made fun of those tele-serials, describing them as "melodramatic, hilarious, and ridiculous", but having Meghna to watch them alongside her was fun.

They left for a trip to Agra and Fatehpur Sikri. The next weekend, they visited Jaipur. The trips were refreshing and enjoyable. The month seemed to pass in a flash. Jyotsna was keen to go with Meghna to Tezpur, but Samar urged her to wait for another two or three months. "It's barely six months since you got here," he said. Jyotsna had no choice but to agree with his rationale. Meghna left for Tezpur alone.

Samar hardly talked to her parents on the phone. Jyotsna did not like his indifference, but she did not say anything.

Did I make a mistake by marrying this man, who is reclusive and unsociable towards my parents?

Her parents wanted a son, not an indifferent son-in-law. Perhaps her mother was right. It may have been better to have married someone from Tezpur or within Assam.

Samar was oblivious to her brooding thoughts. Jyotsna did not make any effort to convey her thoughts to Samar, thinking, *he is supposed to know!*

Meanwhile, in the Civil Services Exams 2007, Vipul cleared all stages and was selected for the IAS on his last attempt. He came over to meet Samar at his office. Samar took him out for a late dinner and drinks. Vipul expected to be allotted his home cadre, MP. His rank was a mind-blowing 32. How unpredictable was the UPSC! After three attempts, he had failed to clear the interview stage, but in his final attempt, he made it with such a high rank!

***

CHAPTER 15

"Maa, I am not feeling well…" Jyotsna called her mother early one morning.

"Oh! What happened? Did you not sleep well at night?" Mrs Deka asked in a concerned voice.

"I slept well, but since morning, I am feeling nauseated and weak…."

"Oh! I hope it's not related to periods?" Mrs Deka asked.

Jyotsna replied hesitantly, "Actually, I have missed my period by 10 days."

"Oh! Why didn't you mention it before? It might be a good sign. Why don't you take a pregnancy test?" Mrs Deka suggested.

"Maa…. I am feeling like vomiting again. I am hanging up… Will talk later."

She disconnected the call abruptly before Mrs Deka could react. She barely managed to reach the bathroom sink before she vomited.

Jyotsna lay down to rest for a while.

She had dozed off for about an hour when she was startled awake by her mother's call.

"How are you feeling now?"

"I am better now, Maa. I fell asleep."

"That's good. Did you take the test?"

"No. I will take it in a while."

"That's okay. Do inform me later.."

Jyotsna found the pregnancy kit in the bathroom cabinet. She sat down to take the test. The strip gradually turned dark, indicating a positive test.

She tried again with a new strip and got a positive reading once more. She checked the expiry date, but it was well within the expiry period.

Her family was elated at the news.

"Let us wait for the result of the ultrasound for confirmation. Let's keep our fingers crossed," Samar said.

Is he not happy?

Samar was in a bad mood after a frustrating day at the High Court and in his office. He appeared in person in the High Court in a matter involving encroachment on Gram Sabha land. He had demolished the encroachment, but the private party had approached the High Court, pleading the demolition as illegal. Samar reached the court much earlier than scheduled and met with the government counsel. The counsel failed to draft a written reply despite being sent proper, para-wise factual comments well in advance. Instead, he took adjournments on three previous dates, which annoyed the court. The counsel briefed him about court etiquette and advised him to plead for leniency. Samar was livid, as he was not at fault.

He waited for about two hours for the case hearing to begin. There were many people, mostly advocates and clients, in the courtroom. When they announced the case number, the judge asked the government counsel, "So, what do you want, Mr Mehra? Your SDM seems to be too busy. He did not bother to come."

"Lordship, I beg your pardon. The SDM is here," Mr Mehra said, looking towards Samar.

The judge eyed Samar with suspicion.

"Mr SDM, you have been wasting this court's precious time. Why haven't you filed the reply?"

"Sir….Your Honour! I beg your pardon. Sorry for the delay!"

"I am not interested in your apology! Tell me, when will you file the reply?"

"Your Honour, I assure you I will file the written reply within three days. I plead for your leniency," Samar answered.

The judge's expression softened.

"Fine. The case is adjourned for two weeks. A written reply should be filed within a week."

Both the counsel and Samar sighed with relief.

Samar returned to his office around lunchtime. Twenty cases were lined up for hearing in the SDM Revenue Court. Samar instructed his Reader to start the court proceedings at 3 pm. The proceedings were interrupted twice as the DM called Samar. Samar did not like such interruptions, but he had no option but to halt proceedings and leave the court. By the time he returned, it was almost 7 pm, and the lawyers for the remaining cases requested an adjournment to another date. Samar granted the same and called it a day.

The next day, they visited a gynaecologist, who confirmed Jyotsna was pregnant. The doctor recommended an ultrasound scan in six to eight weeks and advised rest. Jyotsna took leave for a week.

They went for the ultrasound in the seventh week. The radiologist detected the foetal heart rate and confirmed that the fetus was growing. The gynaecologist advised them to maintain a healthy lifestyle and prescribed certain routine medications. Samar conveyed the good news to his brother's family. Jyotsna's mother gave her several instructions on how to handle the pregnancy and be safe—no heavy lifting, no washing, no squatting…

Jyotsna followed her mother's instructions religiously.

***

One morning, around two months later, Jyotsna noticed a few bloodstains on her innerwear.

Jyotsna ignored them and left for her lab.

When she returned home in the evening, she discovered a much larger reddish patch on her white innerwear. She panicked and immediately called her mother, who suggested seeing a gynaecologist at the earliest. The next day, Samar took her to the same gynaecologist.

"During pregnancy, the menstrual cycle gets suspended. But 20 per cent of pregnant women have spotting during the early pregnancy period," the doctor explained. "Your body is reacting to the suspension of the menstrual cycle. There might be some hormonal imbalances, too."

The gynaecologist smiled reassuringly and said, "This is a little bit of a concern, but it can be resolved easily. I am prescribing progesterone shots during your first trimester. Progesterone is the hormone…"

"I know about progesterone, Doctor," interrupted Jyotsna.

"Good. By the way, how do you commute to work?"

"By bus or auto."

"Well, any travel is strictly prohibited. I advise you to apply for leave and take bed rest. Avoid strenuous physical activities."

They took the doctor's advice seriously. She rested all day, lounging in bed or sitting on the sofa, watching TV, reading a novel, or talking to her parents. She would call Samar once a day, urging him to come home early. They paid the regular maid extra money for the additional work.

Jyotsna had applied for an extended leave from the lab. It was leave without pay, but she did not care.

Samar was concerned, too. He tried to get home early from work. Occasionally, he brought files home instead of sitting till late in the office.

Mrs Barua became a regular visitor during the day, chatting about her son and daughter-in-law in the US, how her son wanted to return to India, but her daughter-in-law hated India. She adored her son but seemed to have little love for the daughter-in-law.

Jyotsna's parents were anxious about her condition. They wanted her to come to Tezpur. Bed rest and a mother's care were the best medicine, they would say. Samar did not like the idea, though.

Two days later, while they were getting ready to sleep, Jyotsna said to Samar, "My father will call you."

" What is it about?" he asked.

"*Deuta* wants to speak to you about taking me to Tezpur."

"It is not a good idea to travel during this time. You need to rest," Samar replied.

"Deuta and Maa said it would be best if I rest all day and stay with them till the delivery."

"You are on bed rest here as well. Delhi has the best medical facilities."

"Yes, but during the daytime, I am all alone. Who will take me to the hospital in case of an emergency?"

"You are overthinking it. Also, the progesterone shots are on schedule. You will be fine. Don't worry!"

"You are not taking it seriously. By the way, Deuta and Maa

were saying they hardly hear from you."

"You know my nature. I can't call people every night, asking what they had for dinner," Samar retorted.

"But close families do," Jyotsna retaliated.

"Let us not get into another fight about family."

Then he added, "The doctor told you not to travel during the first three months. If they are so keen, why don't they stay here till the delivery?"

Jyotsna did not argue further, but she was not convinced. She had more faith in her father's judgement than anyone. If he thought she should be in Tezpur, he must be right. She was like a petulant child when it came to her family.

Samar received a call from Dr Deka the following evening.

"Samar, I need to talk to you," Dr Deka began.

"Sure, Deuta." Samar knew what was coming.

"I understand Delhi is a good place with modern amenities. But we can't stay in Delhi till Jyotsna's delivery. It is better that the delivery is planned at Tezpur."

Samar was silent, trying to hide his displeasure and stay calm. Dr Deka resumed, "Look, son, in our family, a woman delivers her baby at her mother's home."

"Deuta, I would prefer the delivery to be in Delhi. The doctor said it's risky to undertake any travel during the first three months. But if you insist, I will think it over."

"I am a doctor, too."

There was a momentary pause.

"We are coming to Delhi, and would prefer to bring her back with us," declared Dr Deka.

Any further reasoning was pointless since Jyotsna and her parents had already made up their minds.

Jyotsna's parents came to Delhi within a week. Her mother cooked Jyotsna's favourite dishes and fed her well during their short stay. Their flight back was on the coming weekend.

The night before they were to leave, while in bed, Jyotsna tried to convince Samar.

"Samar, everything will be fine. You don't have to worry. Trust my parents."

"You don't trust me!" Samar snapped.

"It is not like that. Deuta is a doctor. They will all be around me there."

"You people have made all the decisions. I don't have any say in the matter."

Samar turned away.

"Nothing untoward will happen," Jyotsna said softly. "I will complete my shots there. Maa will hire a caregiver for me."

Samar looked dispirited.

"Cheer up, Hubby! Today is my last day here for a while. Now give me a little *kissy*," Jyotsna forced a kiss.

Samar cheered up a bit.

"Now promise me you will visit me every month and call me every day."

"I can't promise to come every month, but I will try to talk every day," Samar continued to be sullen.

"I know, my husband is a busy officer." Jyotsna patted him on the back.

They lay down, holding hands.

Unfortunately, things between them became complicated over time. Confusion and mistrust were creeping into their relationship. Samar thought Jyotsna was clingy, assumptive, and dependent. She made her decisions based on self-conceived notions. He detested her parents' interference in their marital lives.

Jyotsna viewed Samar as adamant, careless, aloof, unromantic, and insensitive. He could not live up to her expectations.

***

CHAPTER 16

An unknown number flashed on Samar's mobile screen. He was tempted to ignore it, knowing well that his number was on the public website of the Revenue Department and the Election Department. He switched his phone to vibration mode and lay down on the bed.

Samar had spent a long, tiresome day. The DM held a review meeting on the progress of developmental works under the MPLADS scheme and the status of revenue-related cases in his sub-division. Although a few months had passed since his transfer here, Samar was still struggling to manage the excessive workload.

After another five minutes, the same number flashed again on the screen. Recollecting the words of the Divisional Commissioner, Mrs Nalini Sharma, who once advised the officers of the Revenue Department to be responsive and compassionate to citizens at all times, he picked up the call.

"Hello…. Hello…" It was a familiar female voice, "Am I speaking to Samar?"

"Hello, yes… This is Samar. Who's on the line?"

After a momentary pause, the voice said, "Can you guess?"

In a split second, Samar recognized the voice.

"Abha? Is it Abha?" he asked, his heart racing.

"You recognized me!" Abha exclaimed. "You remember my voice after so many years! That's nice, Samar."

She went on, "Did you ever wonder about me all these years?"

"I did," Samar replied. The past events flashed through his mind.

Samar had come to know much later, through Sunny, that Abha's family had married her off.

"Did you try to find out what happened to me after Zirakpur?" Abha asked.

"I came to know you got married."

"Yes, forcibly," Abha sighed.

"And did you know what happened to me?" Samar asked.

"I am sorry for what happened to you. It's all because of me."

Samar did not respond.

"Thank God you recovered from the terrible incident… and now you are an officer! I am glad, Samar. Your perseverance and dedication paid off."

"Hmm…"

"What happened was beyond our control," she said. "Are you married, Samar?"

"Yes."

"Happy?"

"Why are you asking?"

"Just wondering."

"Are you happy, Abha?"

"I asked you first. You didn't answer my question, Samar."

"Yes, I am married and happy," Samar mumbled. There was a momentary silence.

"That's nice to hear…."

"So, where do you live now, Abha?"

"I am in Delhi. I was wondering if we could meet sometime," Abha suggested.

Samar wondered what to say. He had moved past the 'Abha phase' and did not want to recall the painful memories.

"Samar, there is a lot I want to tell you… So many things you don't know."

"What about your marriage? Are you happy?" Samar asked.

"Happy? I am looking for happiness," Abha chuckled. "I have filed for a divorce."

"What? Why?"

"I will tell you some other time."

***

The next day, Samar wound up his work early and headed home. He tried to dismiss thoughts about Abha from his mind. As the driver drove him to Dwarka, Samar called Jyotsna. It had been two months since she left for Tezpur. The call was picked up after a long ring.

"It's me. How have you been?"

Getting no response, he asked, "Jyotsna, what is the matter?"

"Thank you for asking. I am okay."

Samar could hear the sarcasm in her voice.

"You don't sound that happy, though. What is the matter?" Samar repeated.

"What is the matter? Did you call yesterday to find out how I was doing?" Jyotsna retorted.

"Oh… I was exhausted. I had a busy day yesterday," Samar replied.

"What's new in that? You are always busy. You have loads of work, blah blah blah…"

"Sorry, *Baba*! I will try to call you every day. Now tell me, how are you feeling?"

After a long pause, she said, "I feel exhausted and tired, like you always do."

Samar chuckled and managed to make Jyotsna laugh feebly.

"I have a checkup tomorrow. I wish you were here."

"I wish I could be there, too, but I will need to accumulate earned leaves to be with you during the delivery time."

"I know. I get perturbed and frustrated sometimes. It must be the mood swings."

"Yes, blame it on your mood swings."

"Oh! I am sorry, but you will have to bear with my mood swings."

"Yes, ma'am."

"So, is the maid coming regularly and cooking properly? I hope you warm your food before you eat it."

"Yes, Yes. Everything is fine."

"Do you meet your friend, Sunny?"

"Yes, I met him last Friday for dinner."

"I hope he didn't make you drink too much."

"I didn't, ma'am."

"Okay. We will talk tomorrow. Take care."

"You too. Bye!"

Jyotsna had one or two more episodes of spotting after she left Delhi. Her parents and younger sister looked after her well, but she longed for Samar's support and company. She was in the last phase of her second trimester.

Old memories of Abha and his struggles kept flashing through Samar's mind. He slept poorly that night. The following morning, he did not feel like speaking to Jyotsna and kept himself busy with office work the whole day.

***

A week after her phone call, Abha called again and cajoled Samar to meet for dinner.

"You have to take me out to dinner if you want to know what happened to me after Zirakpur."

They chose a quiet restaurant in Connaught Place. Abha was already seated when he arrived after his office hours. She was nicely dressed and looked as fresh and radiant as ever. Time seemed to have had no effect on her.

"Are officers supposed to look haggard?" Abha teased.

Grinning at the sarcasm, Samar replied, "Not always. I had a long day."

"I ordered a Virgin Mojito for myself. What will you have?" Abha asked.

"Nothing, just water," Samar said to the waiter.

"And any starters, Sir?" the waiter asked.

Eager to dismiss the waiter soon, Samar said, "Just get the vegetable *kebab* platter. We will order the main course in a while."

After the waiter left, Abha said, "This was long overdue." She paused and then continued. "You should know what happened after Zirakpur," she said in a low, melancholy voice, as if reliving those nightmarish moments.

"I heard you entered into holy matrimony with a rich fellow, a matrimony of happiness ever after!" Samar replied.

"Who told you so?"

"Sunny."

"How can you believe such hearsay? Would I be filing for a divorce if I were in 'holy matrimony'?" Abha retorted.

"Oh, I am sorry… I didn't know the reality. Please carry on," Samar said in an apologetic tone.

Abha regained her composure and said, "After they took me to Sonepat that day, they locked me in a room for several days. My family tortured and beat me up… my father, my brother, my uncles…"

Abha's voice trembled as she recounted her ordeal. Samar felt a lump in his throat.

"My mother… my own mother! All she said was, 'They have decided your destiny. Do what they say if you want to stay alive,'" Abha narrated in a dull voice.

"They selected a groom for me, a sitting MLA's son. I kept begging them not to marry me off, but they would not listen. One day, Rohit almost strangulated me, and I fainted. On the wedding day, I was drugged, half-conscious, dressed like a mannequin, dazed…"

"I am so sorry… I had no idea…! How can your own family be so cruel?" Samar's voice was choked.

"And you say, I married happily ever after!" Abha said, tears flowing down her face.

There was a long silence. Samar was horrified at what she had endured.

"Eat the *kebabs*. They will turn cold," Abha said.

They began to eat.

"It's been years now. The physical pain they inflicted on me has gone, but the trauma they etched on my heart will never go away…"

The waiter came to take their order for the main course. After he left, Abha asked, "What happened to you afterwards?"

"I had a serious compound fracture on my right arm, so I had to undergo surgery. I could not appear for the Mains exams and lost one full year."

"Oh, I am so sorry, Samar. I forced you into my ordeal."

The main course arrived.

"How were things with your husband after marriage? What's his name, by the way?"

"Viren. Things were average. We stayed in a large house with my in-laws and his big extended family in Faridabad. We had many servants, luxurious cars, etc." Abha paused before continuing, "But affluence and comfort can never compensate for a loveless marriage… at least, not for long.".

She narrated her story. Viren was indifferent to her. He hardly acknowledged her presence. He expected her to be obedient to his family elders and affable with her sisters-in-law. Abha could not bond with the family, as she had a grudge against them because of the forced marriage. The family was wealthy. Viren's uncle and cousin looked after the family's four jointly owned Ayurvedic drug factories in Solan and Palampur. Viren would also go on long tours, leaving Abha behind at home for several weeks.

After about four years, the joint family had a serious property dispute. A long court battle for the division of the property followed. Meanwhile, Viren's father passed away. One factory came to Viren after his father's death. Viren was the only son, but his two married sisters made claims. Another round of court disputes began. Viren sold a portion of the ancestral property that had come to them, bought a house in South Delhi, and shifted. The family feud between the sisters and Viren was still unresolved in court.

Viren and Abha hardly had any love or bonding between them. Abha could not conceive, as Viren was impotent, but her mother-in-law and others in the family blamed Abha. During one of the many arguments with her mother-in-law, Abha blurted out that her son was impotent. This led to a violent verbal and physical assault by Viren.

The next day, she left the house and rented a room in Rajouri Garden.

It was past 10 pm. Samar and Abha picked at their food during the long monologue.

"You should eat properly, Mr SDM. You have hardly gained much weight after all these years. It seems your wife does not feed you well," Abha joked, trying to lighten the mood.

"I am sorry to hear you have gone through a lot, Abha."

"Leave all this aside. What is your wife's name?" Abha asked.

"Jyotsna."

"That's a beautiful name! Is she Assamese?"

"Yes."

"And beautiful?"

"Yes."

They left the restaurant. On the way back, Abha asked him about the developments in his life. She saw Jyotsna's photos on his mobile. Finally, at 11 pm, Samar dropped her outside her house.

***

CHAPTER 17

The next morning, Samar woke up with a splitting headache. Thoughts about Abha's ordeals had kept him awake for a major part of the night. Old wounds that had supposedly healed seemed to have reopened.

Having forgotten to call Jyotsna the previous night, he was prepared for her sullen mood when he called her up on his way to the office.

"Hi Wifey, any updates from your doctor?" Samar asked.

"Why didn't you call yesterday?"

"I had a long working day. I was tired and slept early."

"You always say the same thing. Anyway, Dr Bora advised me to continue to be on bed rest. The risk is still there," Jyotsna said sadly.

"Do not worry. Just relax. Everything will be fine," Samar assured her.

"I wish you were here with me."

"I will visit you next month."

"That's great. I look forward to it. What did you eat for breakfast? Is Shyama coming regularly?" Jyotsna asked.

"She is a bit irregular these days."

"Why?"

"She says her husband is not well," Samar replied.

"I don't believe her. She is taking advantage of my absence."

"It's okay. I will manage."

Samar sounded uninterested. He instructed the driver to drive faster.

"I think your mind is somewhere else," Jyotsna said accusingly.

"No, I am with you. It's just that I am an adult. I know how to manage."

"Okay, okay! I hope you are not drinking too much with your friends in my absence?"

"No."

"I wish things were different. You are there. I am here. My parents are far more organized than we are."

"Try to relax, and let things happen on their own. Too much planning does not always work. Don't compare our lives with that of your parents."

"Planning worked for them. Anyway, whatever you say, wise man," Jyotsna tried to be humorous but failed. Instead, she sounded irritated.

"I have reached the office. I have to go now. Just relax. Have faith in God."

Samar abruptly disconnected the call, without waiting for a response.

Whenever I talk about my parents, he gets touchy!

Is it my fault that he does not have good family support?

Jyotsna was annoyed with him. She expected him to be more involved in their marriage, but he was always aloof. Samar wished she would understand his nature and behave maturely. She would not have gone to her parents' place for the delivery if she really wanted to be with him. Misunderstandings, misconceptions, and occasional arguments were weakening their relationship.

Samar's Reader reminded him of a written statement draft to be filed with the District Court. But Samar was not in the mood to read. His thoughts continued to wander towards Abha. He did not read the draft and cancelled the Revenue Court.

On his way home, he dialled Abha's number. She did not pick up, but called back 30 minutes later. By that time, Samar was relaxing at home, drinking coffee.

"Hi, how was your day?" she asked.

"Not good."

"Why? What happened?"

"It was just not a good day. Anyway, how was yours?"

"Even mine was not good. My case came up for a hearing today. Viren's lawyer made nasty allegations about my character," Abha replied.

"That's bad. I hate that husband of yours."

"Ex-husband. He is resorting to mudslinging to delay the case and intimidate me. I detest him!"

"You should not get intimidated by that moron."

"I am frustrated with my life. Sometimes, I wish I could die!"

The call got disconnected abruptly.

Samar dialled her back, but the phone was switched off.

Samar became worried that she might do something stupid. He had no option but to wait for her to call back.

She called an hour later.

"Why did you disconnect?" he asked.

"I was feeling low. I don't know why my life has turned out this way. I wanted to be an IAS officer. Instead, destiny…"

"Abha, you got me worked up!"

"I am fighting a case against a powerful man who has loads of black money. My family has abandoned me. I have no one to support me emotionally," she said in a distraught manner. Taking a deep breath, she continued, "I am working in a school, and the salary isn't great. I need money to fight the case. How do you expect me to react?" Her voice broke.

"Just relax. Have faith in God."

He had said the same words to his wife that morning.

Perhaps his wife needed him, too. He felt guilty for not being around for her during this difficult period.

Samar decided to visit Tezpur.

***

During the public hour from 10 am to 11 am, Samar met visitors. A villager had come with a complaint against the Tehsildar for not recording the mutation he sought for a particular piece of land he had inherited. Samar called for the Tehsildar, who offered some lame excuses. Samar chided him and warned him to ensure he recorded the mutation within three days or he would face the music. The villager left happy and reassured.

Another villager sought an update on a case he had filed in the SDM's Revenue Court. Samar instructed the Reader to give an early date in the coming week. A college student requested a time-bound reply to an RTI application. Samar assured him of a reply within the timeframe. A middle-aged widow, with her hands folded and tears in her eyes, requested that her family's ancestral land be correctly demarcated, as she feared the Patwari was being influenced by her two brothers-in-law, who wanted to grab her deceased husband's share. Samar took details of the Khasra numbers of the land and assured her that he would visit the spot on the day of demarcation. She went back relieved.

After the public hour, Samar attended a weekly review meeting called by the DM. The DM reviewed the progress of Revenue Court cases, public grievances, MPLADS and MLALADS works, EPIC card pendency, etc. The DM praised Samar, noting that his performance was better than the other two SDMs. Samar, happy at the rare praise, used the opportunity to submit his earned leave application for 10 days, starting from the first week of the next month.

Samar booked his flight tickets. He heard the Revenue Court case proceedings of the day and cleared a few files. At around 7:30 pm, he called it a day. He rang up Jyotsna.

"Hey, how are you doing?"

"I am fine, Hubby. You seem to be in a cheerful mood today," Jyotsna remarked.

'Yes, I am. I think you are, too."

"Yes. I am in good spirits today."

"Good to hear that. My boss praised my performance today in front of the other SDMs and the district Tehsildars. But that is not the only reason," Samar said.

"Then, tell me."

"Guess..."

"You got your pending pay fixation arrears, maybe?" Jyotsna guessed.

"No." Jyotsna gave up, "Don't test a woman with mood swings! You'd better tell me now!"

"My leave has been approved. I will come to Tezpur on the fifth of next month for 10 days."

"Oh, great! Does this mean my hubby missed me?" Jyotsna teased.

Samar said softly, "Yes, I miss you all the time, Wifey."

"I am happy to hear you say that."

Gladdened by this news, Jyotsna spent the rest of the day thinking about Samar and how much she missed him…

***

The next day, Samar took half a day of casual leave and met Abha after lunch. The government drivers are known to be quite nosy, so he took a cab instead of his official vehicle for privacy. He picked her up and accompanied her to the lawyer, Mr Mathur.

Abha had filed the petition in the Family Court under Section 13 of the Hindu Marriage Act, 1955. Since it was a contested divorce, the court proposed mediation. During the mediation, Viren's lawyer, Jasmine Siddiqui, had hurled wild allegations at Abha and tried to malign her reputation. The court scheduled the case for a hearing after mediation failed. The date given was 20 days later.

Arun Mathur was a young lawyer with eight years of legal practice. They discussed their future strategy. Their original plan was to settle during mediation, assuming Viren would agree to the same. Instead, he accused Abha of stealing his family's antique and expensive jewellery. The divorce hearing seemed headed for an ugly slugfest.

The discussions at the lawyer's chamber ended at about eight in the evening. Samar suggested dinner in Greater Kailash. Abha was initially reluctant but finally agreed.

The diner was crowded. They chose a corner table. Samar ordered Scotch and *Galouti kebabs* while Abha settled for a Pina Colada, her favourite cocktail, and mutton *biryani.*

"Abha, just forget about your divorce issues for this evening," Samar said.

"Then, I need to drown myself in cocktails."

A few drinks helped to divert their minds.

Abha went to the restroom as Samar paid the bill. He took out his cheque book and wrote a cheque in Abha's name for Rs 50,000. He hurriedly put it in her purse before she returned. She would surely refuse to accept it if given directly.

"Viren is such a bastard. He dared to cast aspersions on me in court," Abha vented.

"Yes, he is a real bastard," Samar cursed, the Scotch clearly taking effect.

They burst into wild laughter.

"What about you, Bhabhiji? What should we call you?"

A heavily drunk man was standing at their table.

Abha's face hardened. It was Ashish, Viren's cousin. He could barely stand and clutched the table for support.

"Who are you?" Samar asked.

"Ask Bhabhiji! Who is this man? Bhabhiji? Viren Bhaiya was right. You are a fast woman," Ashish smirked.

"How dare you?" Abha shouted.

Samar caught hold of Ashish's collar. Ashish clenched his fist and aimed a blow at Samar but missed.

"Please, Samar, please don't! It's not worth it. Let's leave this place!" Abha said, alarmed. Samar and Abha started to leave.

"*Oye*! Hero! Wait! You don't know me, you bastard! Who do you think you are?" Ashish shouted.

The bouncer rushed to the table. While he hauled Ashish away, Ashish hurled abuses at them.

Samar and Abha hurriedly left the place, followed by the prying eyes of the other guests.

"Who was that moron?" Samar asked.

"Ashish. He is Viren's cousin. He was part of the joint family. All the men in the family are chauvinistic pigs."

"You must be the first person in the family to have challenged them. It has hurt their inflated ego."

"Hmm…" Abha answered.

Samar reached home late after dropping off Abha.

Before turning in, Samar sent an SMS to Jyotsna: *I was busy with work. Planning to sleep now. Hope you are doing fine.*

Jyotsna: *Carry on! I know you are a busy man. I am fine.*

Jyotsna: *Sleep tight! Miss me! Good night.*

Samar: *Good night.*

He fell asleep soon.

***

The next morning, Samar read another message from Jyotsna: *Hope you are refreshed after a long day, darling! Have a nice day ahead. Call me later, love.*

The endearments in her message both startled and refreshed him. He decided to prepone his trip to Tezpur.

His cell phone beeped. This time, the message was from Abha: *I need emotional support more than monetary help!*

Another beep, another message: *I hope it comes from you.*

What does she mean? Samar wondered.

Her message puzzled him. Abha knew he was married, and his wife was pregnant.

Is she looking for something else from me?

What am I looking for?

***

CHAPTER 18

Samar arrived at Borjhar Airport in Guwahati around noon. The sky was overcast. The taxi took about five hours to reach Tezpur, instead of the usual three and a half hours. The driver blamed the previous night's torrential downpour for the waterlogging on the roads on Guwahati's outskirts. Mid-June is a monsoon month in the Northeast.

Samar arrived at his in-laws' place, exhausted from the flight and the frustrating road trip. Later in the evening, an elaborate spread, including Samar's favourite dishes, was laid out for him. The satisfying dinner restored his spirits.

Jyotsna was in her twenty-sixth week. Her baby bump was big. She had gained weight and looked a few years older than she had in Delhi.

"Are you disappointed by how I look?" Jyotsna asked smilingly.

"No, No. You look lovely."

"Liar!"

"No, I mean it. Of course, you have gained weight, but your radiant smile is still the same."

Jyotsna blushed and smiled.

They slept late, talking, holding hands, and cuddling till late at night. The cuddling took some effort from Samar as the advanced pregnancy made her look like a different person.

The house was a quintessential Assam-style bungalow, spacious and with several rooms, featuring a main wing and a guest wing. Samar's room was in the guest wing. Jyotsna was not around when he was awakened by heavy rain lashing the tin roof the next morning. It was 10:45 am. He forced himself to get up. He spent the next half hour sauntering around leisurely. He was glad of the break from office routine.

The next day, they visited the gynaecologist, Dr Moloya Bora, for a checkup. The doctor seemed satisfied.

"Keep her in good spirits!" he advised Samar.

***

Samar received a few calls from an unknown number on the fourth day after he arrived in Tezpur. He finally responded.

"Hello."

A baritone voice inquired, "Hello, I hope I am speaking to the SDM, Shri Samar, please."

"Yes, Sir. This is Samar."

"Hello. I hope you are doing well. I am Radhey Mohan Munjal, a retired IAS officer."

Samar tried to recall if he had heard the name before.

"I hope you have heard about me before. I have served in various positions, including as a Secretary in the Government of India."

"Sorry, Sir. I might be too junior to you."

"That's possible. I retired in 2007. When did you join the service?"

"Sir, I was undergoing training during that period."

"Then you may not know me. How do you like working in the government?"

"It is a mixed feeling, Sir."

"Yes, I know how it feels. One can do a lot of public good if one is willing, young man."

"Right, Sir."

"So, the reason I called you was because one of my cousins has a case in your court. It has been languishing for a while now."

After a brief pause, he resumed, "You see, the opposite party is crooked. They have been delaying the case in connivance with the lower staff."

"Oh! I see, Sir."

"Can you have a detailed look at the case? I will send my cousin to meet you tomorrow."

"Sure, Sir, but I am currently on leave. I will join next week."

"Oh! Then I will not bother you now. I will call next week."

"Sure, Sir."

Other than that call and another from the DM seeking information, Samar did not receive any other official calls. He was glad of the respite.

***

Abha's case was the first to come up for a hearing in the court that morning. Viren's counsel, Ms Jasmine Siddiqui, carried forward the allegations of the last proceedings. She presented a list of witnesses she wanted to produce before the court. The court allowed it. The first witness was Ashish Joon, Viren's drunkard cousin, whom Abha and Samar had met in the restaurant.

After the introductory questions, Ms Siddiqui moved on to the relevant ones.

"Did you see the petitioner with anyone on the 12th of May this year?" Ms Siddiqui asked.

"Yes, ma'am," he confirmed.

"Where did you see her? Can you elaborate?"

"I saw Abha Bhabhiji with a man on the evening of 12th May at the Black Olive Bar in GK. They were heavily drunk." Ashish looked sheepishly here and there, pretending to be hesitant to reveal further.

"What did you see? Can you describe the scene?" Ms Siddiqui asked.

"They were quite intimate… holding hands like lovers," He paused for a few seconds and then resumed, "Abha Bhabhiji tried to avoid me. That man tried to assault me when I greeted her. Later, they left the place in a hurry."

"What makes you think they are involved? He might just be a friend," Ms Siddiqui said.

"Arrey, Madam. Do friends hold hands in a public place? The way they were looking at each other, they can't be friends."

Abha flushed with anger.

"That's all, Your Honour! Mr Mathur can cross-examine him now," Ms Siddiqui said, glancing towards Arun Mathur, Abha's counsel. He rose to cross-examine the witness.

"How did you assume they were more than just friends?" Mr Mathur questioned.

"They were holding hands in a public place," Ashish replied curtly.

"You assumed them to be lovers just because they were holding hands? Can't a friend hold his friend's hand to console them?"

The question flustered Ashish a bit, but he regained his composure and recited practised lines. "In our society, and specifically in our family, women do not visit a bar. They do not meet friends in restro-bars. They do not hold hands in public. They do not drink in public places. In my limited worldly experience, they appeared to be nothing but lovers. Pardon my limited experience," he said with feigned righteousness.

"Your Honour! How can one assume that two friends sitting in a bar, having dinner and conversing, are lovers, unless one has a feudal mentality? A witness with such an outlook cannot be admitted. That's all, Your Honour!"

Ms Siddiqui returned to address the court again as Arun Mathur went back to his seat.

"Your Honour! My next witness is Mr Vinay Talwar."

Abha could hardly recognize Vinay Talwar, the property dealer in Old Rajendra Nagar, after so many years. Vinay had lost most of his hair. He had a prominent double chin and a belly bulge.

"Mr Talwar, what do you do?" Ms Siddiqui began his examination.

"I am a property dealer. We buy and sell properties, you see... Renting, too," answered Vinay nervously.

"Do you know Abha Deswal?" Ms Siddiqui asked.

"Yes. I remember her. She came many years ago to Rajendra Nagar to prepare for the IAS. I helped her find rented accommodation," Vinay recollected.

"Do you know a person called Samar Sarma?" Ms Siddiqui showed him a photograph of Samar.

"Yes, it is him. Samar. He was from the Northeast. A shy, quiet fellow."

"Good. What do you know about Samar?"

"Samar took a rented accommodation through my dealership. He came to prepare for the IAS," Vinay replied.

"Do you recall whether Samar Sarma and Abha Deswal knew each other?"

"Yes, ma'am, they knew each other rather well," Vinay flashed a mischievous smile as he answered.

"Can you throw some light on the nature of the relationship between Samar Sarma and Abha Deswal back then?"

"I think they were involved."

"Anything specific? Were they seen together?"

"Yes. Initially, they went around a lot. Coffee or tea stalls, walking to classes. I think they were more than friends. Later, they probably drifted apart."

"What do you mean by 'they drifted apart'?" Ms Siddiqui prodded.

"Abha Deswal is a beautiful girl. Anyone would fall for her," he said, looking at the judge.

He continued, "Punit also dated her for a while."

"Who is Punit?" Ms Siddiqui asked.

Bastards! Vinay Talwar, Punit, all of them are bastards! I hate them!

Abha's heart thumped so loudly, she feared even the judge might hear it.

"Punit Oberoi is my cousin. He is now into the export-import business. I introduced him to Abha Deswal. They were quite an item for about a year," Vinay grinned slightly.

"Your Honour! Point to be noted. The petitioner had quite a reputation!" said Ms Siddiqui.

"What more can you tell the Hon'ble court?" she asked.

"I once booked a hotel room for Punit and Abha."

"What is the relevance of my petitioner's past with the case, Your Honour?" objected Mr Mathur.

"Your Honour, it has relevance. We will come to that in a while."

"Objection overruled!" said the judge.

"Why did you book the hotel room?" asked Ms Siddiqui.

"They came late from a party and spent the night together. I had booked rooms for them on a few more occasions also."

Abha felt exposed. Her reputation, honour, and self-respect were at stake. She felt sick and wished she could become invisible.

"After Punit, did she resume her affair with Samar Sarma?"

"Yes, madam. I think Abha and Samar were back together. Late one night, Samar booked a taxi from Talwar Travels to Chandigarh. We have a taxi business also… Business diversification, you see."

"Please restrict your answer to what I ask, Mr Talwar," Ms Siddiqui reprimanded him.

"Go on, Mr Talwar. The court does not have time for your pauses," the judge said. Vinay folded his hands in apology and said, "Sir, Lord! Samar and Abha eloped to Chandigarh that night. Abha's brother came to my office around dawn with some goons. He forced me to reveal the address at Zirakpur to where they had fled." *So… You spoilt my life, you bastard!* There was a momentary silence in the court. Ms Siddiqui took a long breath and summarized, "Your Honour, the testimonies of the two witnesses point to the fact that Abha Deswal had quite a reputation prior to her marriage to my client, Mr Viren Joon. She is a pretty woman who knows how to take advantage of her looks. She enticed Mr Samar Sarma and had a full-fledged affair with him during her stint in Delhi for about two years. She had an affair with Mr Punit Oberoi, too, as my witness narrated. She used to spend time at fancy restaurants, trendy pubs, etc., with Mr Oberoi. Later, when she broke up with him, she rekindled her affair with Mr Sarma. She even eloped to Chandigarh with him," Ms Siddiqui paused momentarily, glancing at Abha, who had her face down.

"Throughout the time she was with my client, she never accepted him as her husband. She did not love him or respect his family. She never invested in the marriage. She left his house, returned to Delhi, and revived her affair with Mr Samar Sarma. She has been spotted in public places with him."

Abha could barely hold back her tears. Ms Siddiqui went on, "Your Honour, my client wants to plead that despite her flaws, past behaviour, and affairs, he and his family are ready to accept Abha back into their family. He wants to give this marriage another chance." Abha's counsel looked alarmed about the day's proceedings. He pleaded for another date for further arguments.

"Further hearing is adjourned till 20th July," said the judge.

Abha was glad Samar was not present in the court. He would have been appalled to hear the ugly allegations.

***

CHAPTER 19

Eight days of Samar's visit to Tezpur had passed. Jyotsna's spirits were high. Despite the advanced stage of pregnancy, physical exhaustion, anxiety, and mood swings seemed to have vanished from the day Samar had arrived. Samar was also in good spirits.

On the evening before Samar's departure, a number flashed on his mobile. Jyotsna disconnected the call as Samar was in the bathroom. The number flashed again almost instantly. Jyotsna picked up the call.

"I am feeling lonely and sad, Samar. When will you come back?" said a distraught female voice.

Without waiting for a response, the woman continued, "I miss you. Viren's lawyer maligned me in court today. He linked us. I am very upset. When will you be back? I need you..."

On receiving no response, the lady said anxiously, "Are you there, Samar? Samar! What is the matter?"

Jyotsna did not know what to say. She kept quiet. The woman disconnected the call, sensing something was wrong. Jyotsna saw that the caller's name was Abha.

Who could this Abha be? Samar has never mentioned her before.

Jyotsna did not mention the call to Samar, but it disturbed her immensely. Abha's words echoed in her ears the entire evening. Finally, she retired to bed, upset and disheartened.

Samar might be involved with the woman; otherwise, how could she expect so much from him?

***

The next day, Jyotsna was in a low mood. Tears ran down her flushed cheeks as Samar was leaving. She felt she was probably losing him to another woman. She cried for the future of their baby.

Samar was oblivious of the doubts and suspicions in Jyotsna's mind. He tried to console her and assured her he would be back at the time of the delivery.

Half an hour after Samar left for Guwahati Airport, he received a call from an unknown number.

"Hello, is this Mr Samar's number?" a male voice asked.

"Yes. This is Samar. May I know who is on the line?" Samar answered.

"Sir, I am calling from the SHO's office, Rajouri Garden Police Station. Sir, do you know someone named Abha Deswal?"

"Yes, why?"

He was puzzled. He had not spoken to her while in Tezpur.

"Sir, Ms Abha has been in the hospital since early morning. Her flatmate found her unconscious in her room. The landlord and the roommate rushed her to the hospital," replied the man.

"Who are you? Is Abha fine? How did you find me?" shouted Samar.

"Sir, I am Constable Pramod Yadav. My SHO asked me to call you since you were the last person she called yesterday evening. Madam Abha Deswal has taken an overdose of sleeping pills. Fortunately, she was brought to the hospital on time."

"Oh my God! Where is she? Is she fine now?"

"She is in Mata Sundari Devi Memorial Hospital," replied Pramod.

"Oh! I see. But I did not receive her call yesterday. You must be mistaken," said Samar.

"Sir, we have confirmed it. She called you yesterday evening. She asked for you this morning. Sir, are you the SDM, Kapashera?"

"Yes, I am. I am on the way from Guwahati to Delhi and will reach tonight."

"Very well, Sir. I just wanted to inform you."

Pramod disconnected the call. Samar called Abha's mobile, but it was switched off. He then called Jyotsna.

"Hello, how are you?"

"I am okay. Where have you reached?" asked Jyotsna.

"I have crossed Dhekiajuli town. Listen, did someone named Abha Deswal call on my mobile yesterday evening?"

How did he find out? Abha must have told him.

Hearing Abha's name further dampened her already low spirits.

"Tell me! Did you pick up a call from Abha?"

"Yes, I did," replied Jyotsna in a dispirited voice.

"Why didn't you tell me, then?" Samar asked.

Jyotsna fumbled to find an excuse. "I forgot. I thought it was not important."

"No, it was very important."

Jyotsna could hear the agitation in his voice.

"Oh! I am sorry, then. I did not know she was so important. I should have told you."

"Yes. You should have!" Samar scolded her.

Jyotsna disconnected the call, enraged.

Samar was angry that he could not pick up Abha's call. She might have wanted to tell him something that was bothering her, something that might have driven her to the sleeping pills.

He redialled Jyotsna's number.

"Why did you disconnect the call? What did Abha say?" Samar asked in an agitated tone.

"She said, 'I am missing you, Samar! When will you be back?'" Jyotsna mimicked.

Samar remained silent.

"Explain to me, Samar, what was I supposed to say? That your Abha was missing you?" said Jyotsna hysterically.

"What nonsense! There is nothing like that, Jyotsna. You are misjudging the situation."

Jyotsna was further enraged and almost shouted, "Oh! I am misjudging. She was longing for your love and company, and you say, I am misjudging!"

"I will tell you everything. Just be patient. Don't misunderstand me."

"Then, why don't you clear my misunderstanding?"

"You are overreacting."

"I am not overreacting. You are hiding something from me."

"I don't have time for all this drama now."

"Oh! So, now I am doing drama. Very well. Let it be."

"Jyotsna, please understand. Abha is an old friend. She is in the hospital because of an overdose of sleeping pills. I am about to reach the airport. I will speak to you later," Samar tried to explain calmly.

"I don't feel like talking right now. Goodbye," Jyotsna said and disconnected without waiting for an answer.

Samar's concern and anxiety for Abha, and his lack of understanding of Jyotsna's feelings, doubts, and suspicions, made her suspicious. She spent the entire day in bed, sobbing and feeling jealous, despondent, and hopeless about the future.

***

During his flight, Samar tried to call Abha a few times, but her mobile remained switched off. His argument with Jyotsna irritated him. His mind was preoccupied with Abha's attempted suicide and what might have led her to take such a step.

He arrived in Delhi late at night. He was still angry with Jyotsna and did not want to talk to her. So, he merely dropped her a message about his safe arrival. He reached home and tried calling Abha again. Exhausted from the journey, he fell asleep within 15 minutes of lying down on the bed.

The next morning, he saw a message from Jyotsna: *Wake up, husband! I know you must be glad to be back in Delhi. Hope your friends are glad too.* Samar recognized the sarcasm in the message.

Ignoring the message, he rushed to the hospital. He found Abha's room and sat down by her bed. There was silence for a while.

Then he asked, "Why did you take the pills?"

"I felt helpless and lonely… Give me some time. I will be fine."

"You scared me, Abha. This is not done."

"Don't worry, Samar. I am much better now."

"Please promise me you will never do such a thing again."

It took Abha a while to say, "I promise."

Samar sat by her side, holding her hands. She narrated the last court proceedings, the character assassination, the allegations about an affair with Samar during her preparation days and that she had rekindled the affair. She had been in low spirits, and had called him.

"I felt lonely… no one loved me, no one cared for me! My life seemed worthless. So, I took those pills..." Her voice broke, and her body shook while tears streamed down her face.

Samar tried to comfort her, "Never think like that! You are not alone. I will be by your side whenever you need me. It's a promise."

"Thank you for being there for me," Abha squeezed his hand. "Cheer up now. You need to relax, too."

"Got it, ma'am!"

Abha glanced at Samar. She recollected the old times in Rajendra Nagar during their IAS preparation days. She genuinely regretted hurting him back then. But Samar was as pure, selfless, and loyal as ever and did not hold any grudge. Instead, he was trying to help her as much as he could. She wished it were like old times and that Samar were available…

***

CHAPTER 20

A fortnight after Samar returned from Tezpur, Sunny called him at 7 am. It was odd for Sunny to call so early.

Still sleepy, Samar picked up the call, yawning. "Hey Sunny, so early in the morning…"

"Hey, Samar, sorry to bother you so early…" Sunny's voice sounded serious.

"What is the matter? Anything wrong, buddy?"

Sunny was an additional DCP in Central Delhi.

"I am afraid I have bad news for you," Sunny said in a low voice.

Samar felt his heart thumping hard.

"Samar! Are you there?" Sunny asked.

"Er… yes…" Samar managed.

"Today, early morning, we found a young woman hanging from the ceiling fan of her house… dead!" Sunny said. After a pause, he continued, "I am afraid you know her."

"Who is it?" Samar asked feebly.

Is it Abha?

"Shraddha…" Sunny replied.

"What? Shraddha? Shraddha Mittal? Oh my God! This is shocking!"

"She left a suicide note."

"The Mittals are responsible for her death!" Samar almost shouted.

"Well, her note implicated their role."

"Oh God! This is very sad."

"I can understand, Samar… I can send you the note… in case you want to see it," Sunny said in a consoling voice.

After a pause, Samar said, "Yes, send it."

"I just wanted you to know, Samar."

"You must punish them. They are responsible for her death."

"We will do our best."

"Hmmm."

Sunny ended the call.

Shraddha had committed suicide in the same room where Samar stayed for a few months at the Mittals'. The postmortem report confirmed suicide by hanging. Shraddha's suicide note mentioned the long period of physical, mental, and emotional torture for dowry she had undergone. Social pressures and compulsions prevented her from reporting the matter to the police. Her note also mentioned that her father had somehow arranged 20 lakhs for the Mittals, thinking the demands would stop. However, their demands had continued. She had begged and pleaded with them, but they tortured her. Shraddha was broken and traumatized, living in fear and agony. She wanted the torture to end. She had lost the motivation to live, and ending her life was the only escape she could think of. Shraddha's final words were: *I want to be at peace and rest forever.*

Shraddha's suicide was widely covered by the local news channels. The police were under a lot of pressure. A day after the incident, Samar saw in the news that the Mittals were arrested on charges of dowry harassment and abetment to suicide based on the suicide note, and the deposition of the servants and maids. On interrogation, the servants reported physical torture the night before Shraddha's suicide.

Samar kicked himself for not checking on Shraddha or offering her any help. He felt he could have somehow helped her, especially after becoming an officer. If only he had not been so preoccupied with his professional life and had tried to reconnect with Shraddha, maybe she would have been alive…

The incident kept Samar in low spirits for many days. Shraddha's suicide continued to captivate the media, which repeatedly broadcasted clips of the Mittals' arrest and sound bites of Shraddha's grieving family demanding justice.

However, after about a fortnight, Shraddha faded from public and media memory.

***

Samar had been meeting Abha regularly. The police did not press any charges against her. She told the police she had an accidental overdose of sleeping pills and that it would not happen again. Having Samar in an influential position helped.

Samar was in the food court of a popular mall in Rajouri Garden, eating breakfast with Abha, when his phone rang.

"Hello, am I speaking to Mr Samar, the SDM of Kapashera?" a firm, urgent male voice said.

"Yes, I am Samar, the SDM," replied Samar.

"Sir, I am a lawyer, Alok Mishra. I want to meet you on an urgent and confidential matter. Sir, at what time can I meet you today?"

"I am away from the office, but I will arrive around noon."

"Not an issue, Sir. I will come to your office around 12:15 pm then."

Alok Mishra arrived on time. He worked in a criminal law firm on Malcha Marg and with *Khilta Bachpan*, an NGO working against child labour.

He came straight to the point. "Sir, are you aware of the child labour going on in your area?"

"Nothing has come to my notice lately."

"Well, Sir, child labour is going on right under your nose."

"We will conduct rescue operations if we come across any cases of child labour in our sub-division. Can you be more specific?" Samar asked.

"I received a tip-off that there is an illegal factory running in Goyla Khurd with child labour."

"Is your tip-off reliable?"

"My source is reliable. I urge you to conduct a rescue operation as soon as possible," Mr Mishra said.

"Okay, I have to bring the matter to my DM."

Samar briefed the DM, Prabhat Ranjan, about the child labour in Goyla Khurd. Mr Mishra had told him that relatives of a former MLA were running the factory.

"We can crack down on the factory if you are sure about the tip-off. But we have to plan the rescue operation meticulously. We can plan it for tomorrow," Mr Ranjan said.

"Right, Sir," Samar nodded.

"But how come an NGO is informing you? Were you not aware of it?"

"Sir, I was not aware. I will do a thorough survey of the area again soon," Samar said.

"Okay, but you must keep your eyes and ears open to what goes on in your sub-division."

"Right, Sir."

"Meanwhile, for this rescue, I want a properly planned operation. Contact the area ACP, Labour department, etc. Take this NGO along. There should be no mistake or media embarrassment later."

Samar assured him that he would do his best.

Samar sat with Alok Mishra and planned the details of the rescue operation. He set aside all other work for the day.

On the way back home that evening, Samar talked about the day's events with Jyotsna.

"Best of luck for tomorrow, Hubby," Jyotsna said. "How is your friend, Abha?"

"She is recovering. She has suffered a lot in life."

Jyotsna heard the softness in his voice when he mentioned Abha.

"Carry on with your wonderful work, both on the professional and personal front. You are a good friend," said Jyotsna. Samar smiled.

He had told Jyotsna that Abha was going through bitter divorce proceedings and that he was helping her as a close friend. However, Jyotsna was not convinced. She suspected an affair between them. Samar was oblivious to the suspicion, mistrust, and tumult in Jyotsna's mind.

***

The next day, at around 9 am, the various teams were ready for the operation. The SDM team included the Tehsildar, the area Patwari, the Reader, 15 civil defence volunteers, a few CDV wardens, Alok Mishra, and two personnel from *Khilta Bachpan*. The police team was led by the area ACP and comprised the SHO and eight constables, including four female constables. The team from the Labour department comprised the District Labour Officer and the Labour Inspector. Samar had also summoned a medical team consisting of a male and a female doctor and their assistants. All of them assembled outside the identified factory in Goyla Khurd.

It stood at the corner of an unauthorized colony. The building was obscure and didn't appear as though a factory would be operational on the premises. The police team and the CDVs surrounded the premises from all sides. Samar's team and the NGO personnel entered from the front entrance while the ACP's team entered from the side entrance.

The sudden appearance of khaki-uniformed personnel frightened the inmates. Inside the dimly lit hall, children were engaged in making packets. The supervisor, a sprightly, slender fellow, shivering with fear, did not know how to handle the situation. The children shrieked and tried to run towards the exit gate. The NGO personnel swung into action. They lined up the children, boys and girls, in separate rows. There were 12 boys and six girls, ranging in age from six to about 14 or 15. Apart from the hall, there were stores for storing the raw material and finished products, dirty common toilets, a hall on the first floor for lunch, a dingy, dimly lit kitchen, and the supervisor's office. On interrogation, the supervisor admitted that they had no work permit, Labour Department permit, etc.

Samar and the NGO personnel tried to pacify the children and served them water. A six-year-old girl, the youngest among them, was badly frightened. Samar patted her head.

"Beta, aap ka naam batao. Darro mat," he said in a soft voice.

The girl hesitated and looked at the supervisor.

"Darro nahin, beta."

"Roshni," she replied in a barely audible voice.

The entire operation lasted for about four hours. The team recorded the children's names and home addresses. Photographs were taken. Snacks and water bottles were arranged for the children. Samar escorted the bus carrying the rescued children to two Children's Homes, where they were to be temporarily lodged.

Details of the owner of the premises were recorded. A seizure memo and a disclosure memo were drafted. The DM and the District Child Welfare Committee members were informed. It was late evening when they concluded the operation. They registered an FIR late in the night against the owner, who was the brother-in-law of a former MLA. The factory was sealed.

"Outstanding work, Samar! Be alert for the follow-up actions," the DM remarked over the phone.

The next day, they produced the rescued children before the Child Welfare Committee. The CWC directed the police to conduct inquiries into the employment documents and to collect the muster roll, the children's statements, and photos of the workplace for prosecution. The CWC recommended medical examinations to determine the age of the children and any case of child abuse. Counselling by social workers and counsellors, as well as legal aid by the District Legal Services Authority, was coordinated by Samar and his team.

During the next few days, Samar was busy with post-rescue operations. The CWC individually interviewed and counselled each child. The District's Child Welfare Officer drafted a report. The CWC ensured advertisements and publicity for the parents to come forward and claim their child. Children whose parents were identified were sent back to them. Such parents were counselled. There were a few children whom no one claimed. Roshni was one of them. These children were sent to a Children's Home.

Jyotsna's family narrated the crucial role Samar played in the rescue and post-rescue operations to every relative in Tezpur. Jyotsna's heart swelled with pride.

***

About a fortnight later, Samar was eating breakfast when Abha's name flashed on his mobile.

"Where were you busy for the past fortnight? No reply or response," Abha said. Over the last few weeks, Abha had gradually regained her spirits.

"I was busy with work."

"Yes, I saw your name in the newspaper. You conducted a child labour rescue operation."

"Yes, it was a tiresome, long procedure. It was heartbreaking to see such young children affected by poverty, neglect, and a lack of basic rights..."

"Tell me in detail," Abha said.

Samar narrated the rescue operation, post-rescue investigations, and ongoing rehabilitation efforts. Abha listened with interest.

Then she said, "I called to tell you that the next date for the hearing of my case is next week on 20th July."

"I see."

"Will you be able to attend it? I am not aware of court matters. You, being from the government, will have a better idea."

"Okay, I will try to attend."

That afternoon, Mr Radhey Mohan Munjal, the retired officer who had called Samar when he was in Tezpur, telephoned him. Samar's PA transferred the call.

"Namaskar, Sir. How have you been?" Samar greeted him.

"I am fine. Thank you. I hope you are fine, too," replied Mr Munjal.

"Sir, please tell me, how can I help?"

"Mr Samar, there is a Land Revenue case in your court. The title is 'Gram Sabha Rewla Khanpur vs Harender Gupta and Ors.'. The case is simple. The party has had the land for a long time. I don't know why the Gram Sabha has registered a false case in your court. I request you to expedite the case and issue the order in favour of the private party."

"I have to hear the case and know the facts, Sir."

"Of course! Hehe... of course! You must complete all the formalities. Just try to issue the order soon. The private party has been harassed for long."

"I will try my best, Sir."

Samar jotted down the case title and asked the Reader to bring him the case file.

***

CHAPTER 21

The case "Abha Deswal vs Viren Joon" flashed on the electronic board of the courtroom. It was the last item for the day. Ms Siddiqui, Viren, and Ashish, his cousin, were present from the respondent's side. Abha and Mr Arun Mathur, the counsel, were present from the petitioner's side. Samar was also present, seated a few benches from the front row. As the last hearing had been unfavourable for his client, Abha's counsel changed their strategy, saying, "We should go on the offensive."

Mr Arun Mathur got up to plead, his body language confident.

"Your Honour, I want to invite the petitioner, Ms Abha, to the examination box," he said.

"Granted," said the judge.

Abha walked to the witness box. She looked nervous and unsure.

"Ms Deswal, could you tell the Honourable Court how old you are?" asked Mr Mathur.

"I am 29," Abha said.

"How long have you been married?"

"About six years now."

"How was your marriage and husband's household?"

"It was an arranged marriage. My in-laws had a large family. Apart from my in-laws, there were uncles, aunts, sisters-in-law, brothers-in-law… I tried hard to fit in but failed…"

"Please carry on," the counsel said encouragingly.

"We lived in a large house as a joint family. It was a typical patriarchal setup. It was difficult to please everyone in the family, particularly my mother-in-law. She was very dominating. My husband used to go on long business trips…" Abha recited the practised lines.

"You mean, your husband was away, leaving you at home," her counsel interrupted, as planned.

"Yes."

"What was the frequency of his trips?"

"It was twice or thrice a month, and each trip lasted about a week."

"You mean, your husband was away for a major part of the month, leaving you behind."

"Yes. He was at home only for about 8 to 10 days a month."

Ms Siddiqui rose to object. "Your Honour, Mr Mathur is taking too much of the Honourable Court's time in this long narrative."

"Your Honour, these are important details," said Mr Mathur.

"Your Honour, I wonder what the learned counsel is trying to prove. Are these details relevant to the case?" Ms Siddiqui interjected.

"I think they are important," the judge said. "Mr Mathur, please carry on."

"Thank you, Your Honour."

Looking at Abha, Mr Mathur asked, "Did you go with Mr Viren on his trips sometimes? Did he take you, or did you ever insist on accompanying him?"

"He allowed me to accompany him only twice. I would insist, but he always said, 'What will you do when I am busy with my work? Women in our house don't go on work trips. Stay back.'"

"How was your relationship with your husband?"

Abha looked embarrassed. She remained silent.

"Ms Deswal, this is important. Please answer the question."

Abha took a deep breath and resumed, "There was hardly any relationship." She felt exposed before the court and looked down. The judge became attentive. Ms Siddiqui looked upset. She did not like the direction in which the case was moving.

"Was there any violence involved?"

"He hit me a few times."

Abha looked visibly embarrassed. She glanced at the audience to find Samar seated in the fourth row, his eyes on her.

"You mean to say, your husband was violent?"

"Yes."

"Is there anything more you would like to add?"

"He hardly spent time with me. Whenever he was home, he would have drinking sessions with his cousins till late at night.

Afterwards, he would come to our room, seeking to satisfy his desires. He had no emotional connection with me. He would hardly acknowledge me as a human being. He expected me to be an obedient doormat…" Tears rolled down her cheeks as she recollected those hard times, "In fact, it was better when he was away on his business trips. At least, I could live without fear when he was away…"

There was silence in the courtroom. Viren and his cousin smirked, while Ms Siddiqui shook her head in despair.

"Ms Abha, can you please elaborate on your physical relationship with Mr Viren? Why was violence involved?" her counsel nudged her.

"I dreaded his touch… He would slap me, push me, violate me in bed as if I was an object, not a living being…" Abha's voice cracked. She was unable to control her emotions.

"Why was he violent with you in bed?"

"He would abuse me, saying I could not give him a child. My mother-in-law and all the other aunts in the family would blame me for not being able to conceive…" Abha's eyes met Viren's. She shuddered at the hatred in his eyes.

"Ms Abha, please continue."

"My mother-in-law called me names. My husband vented his frustration on me, but in reality, it is not me who is at fault… not me… it is him! He is impotent!" Abha's pitched voice rose to a crescendo.

There were murmurs in the courtroom. Abha looked at Viren boldly. She was not afraid anymore. Samar was shocked to hear about Abha's trials.

The judge looked sympathetic. Mr Mathur looked triumphant and relaxed, while Ms Siddiqui looked confused and disturbed. She hurried to arrange a date to cross-examine Abha. The court adjourned the case for two weeks.

***

Samar began to read the case file of 'Gram Sabha, Rewla Khanpur vs Harender Gupta and Ors'. Harender Gupta had bought two *bighas* of agricultural land in Rewla Khanpur from one Vijender Tyagi and had applied for a mutation in his name before the *Tehsildar*, who recorded the mutation in Harender Gupta's name. The Gram Sabha, Rewla Khanpur, challenged the mutation, and the Gram Sabha counsel lodged the case in SDM Kapashera's court. The document on which Harender Gupta claimed the mutation was a Power of Attorney signed by him and Vijender Tyagi.

The SDM's court upheld the mutation. Thereafter, the Gram Sabha filed an appeal against the SDM's court order in the DM's court, claiming the land to be Gram Sabha land. The case was transferred to the ADM by the DM.

Samar found the way Mr Munjal had tried to influence him to decide in favour of Harender Gupta doubtful and decided to probe deeper into the case. He called for old revenue records from the BDO office. He found that the land in question was Gram Sabha land, and Vijender Tyagi had illegally encroached upon it. He had no modus operandi to sell the Gram Sabha land.

***

One evening, Jyotsna was alone at home. Her parents and Meghna had gone to attend a function in the neighbourhood. Feeling lonely and melancholy, she took a stroll in the courtyard, her mind occupied with thoughts of Samar and Abha.

The maid had watered the plants, and there was water on the ground. As Jyotsna took a step forward, her right foot slipped on the floor of the courtyard. She desperately grabbed a branch of a Bougainvillaea shrub. The thorns pricked her palm. Her left foot could not support her weight and slipped, too. The branch of the shrub broke off, and Jyotsna fell on a flower pot. The pot crumbled under her weight and toppled sideways, knocking Jyotsna off balance. She landed on her belly with a heavy thud.

Jyotsna groaned in pain. Blood oozed from the bruises on her right palm. She felt a pulsating pain in her abdomen. There were blood spots on her clothes. She panicked, anticipating internal injury to the baby. She called out, "Anyone nearby, please help me! Help me!"

There was no one around. Stretching out her left hand, she managed to reach her mobile, which was thrown a few feet away. She frantically dialled Meghna and then her father, but they did not pick up the call.

She dialled Samar's number. After a long ring, a woman picked up the call.

"Hello, who is there?"

"Samar! Samar! Can I speak to Samar?"

"Samar is in the washroom. Let me call him." She heard the woman calling out to Samar. Jyotsna could hear Samar's reply in the background.

"I am not cleaned up, baby! Who is it, Abha?" Samar shouted out.

"Ssshhh… I think your wife is on the line," Abha said, lowering her voice, though it was still audible over the phone.

After a brief pause, Samar came on the line. "Hello, Jyotsna… tell me, anything urgent?"

"I had a nasty fall. I think the baby is hurt. I think my water broke!" Jyotsna shrieked hysterically.

"Oh my God! How did you fall? Where are your parents?"

"Oh my God… I think my baby is going to come out!" shouted Jyotsna.

The mobile fell from her hands. Jyotsna cried for help, "Help me! Help me, anyone!"

No one could hear her voice…

Jyotsna woke up suddenly, sweating profusely. She felt her heart thumping hard. She realized she was in her bed. Meghna was in a deep sleep next to her. She checked the table clock; it was 3:30 am. It was a bad dream, a scary, horrific dream…

Jyotsna was in the thirty-third week of her pregnancy. Negative thoughts about the safety of her delivery, Samar's suspected affair with Abha, and his indifference towards her feelings weighed on her mind, leading to mood swings. She could not share her thoughts with anyone, not even her sister. She drank water from the copper vessel next to her bedside and lay down. Sleep was elusive. She finally managed to sleep in the wee hours of the morning.

The next day, she narrated her dream to Samar over the phone. "You are nervous about the delivery," explained Samar. "It is natural to worry since it is our first baby. But don't worry. Everything will be fine."

"I am scared… terrified! And you don't even bother."

"You are overthinking, wifey. Relax!"

"You are taking care of your friend, Abha, there. What about me? Who will take care of me?" Jyotsna asked. Samar fought to control his temper. He was fed up with counselling her all the time.

"You have your parents and sister. That's why you left for Tezpur. I would have taken care of you in Delhi, but you did not listen to me," Samar retorted.

"But I need my husband with me, too."

"I have to work. I have responsibilities."

"I know what responsibilities you are upholding," argued Jyotsna.

"Don't fret, Jyotsna. You preferred Tezpur to Delhi. As for Abha, she is a friend who needs emotional support as she is going through a messy divorce. How many times do I have to clarify this to you?" Samar snapped, irritated.

"You don't understand, Samar!" Jyotsna's voice began to crack. There was silence for about half a minute, after which Jyotsna broke into a whimper.

This mellowed down Samar a bit. He tried to console her. "Jyotsna, don't cry. I want my wife to be emotionally strong, not someone who is always whining."

"Leave it! You never support me. I will talk to you later," Jyotsna said and ended the call.

Samar did not call her back. He was not in the mood.

***

CHAPTER 22

Abha's deposition during the previous hearing had a major impact. It affected the Joon family immensely. Abha's statement leaked to their social circle and business rivals, causing them huge embarrassment. Ms Siddiqui had earlier advised Viren that Abha had valid grounds for divorce and that an out-of-court settlement was the easier option. The patriarchs of the family persuaded Viren to stop squabbling in court and settle the divorce as early as possible, by whatever means necessary. Some sane voices in the family even blamed Viren for being unreasonable and indifferent towards Abha while they were together.

Viren reluctantly instructed his counsel to discuss with Abha's counsel about an out-of-court settlement. The counsels arranged a meeting in a conference room in the basement of Ms Siddiqui's law firm office at Neeti Bagh.

"Mr Mathur, your client acted well on that last occasion. The court loved the melodrama and the histrionics," Ms Siddiqui began with a mocking smile.

"Ms Siddiqui, come to the point. I am not interested in your jibes," Mr Mathur retorted.

Viren Joon and two of his cousins, Ashish and Anshul, were seated next to Ms Siddiqui. Abha and Mr Mathur were seated across the oval-shaped sturdy mahogany conference table.

"Please don't get me wrong for appreciating Ms Abha's theatrical skills. She played well to the galleries without bothering about her reputation. But my clients are respectable people," Ms Siddiqui said.

Abha flushed at the snide remarks.

"Ms Siddiqui, my client also has her reputation at stake."

"Huh!" Ms Siddiqui smirked.

"Ms Siddiqui, your client's atrocities and attitude forced my client to file for a divorce. We wanted to settle mutually, but your client was adamant to contest the divorce," Mr Mathur said. "We will leave if you continue to pass snide remarks about my client." Mr Mathur and Abha stood up and started walking away.

"Oh, come on. Please come back," Ms Siddiqui softened. As Mr Mathur and Abha sat down, she continued, "Very well, Mr Mathur. My client, Mr Viren Joon, is wary of going to court. He has better things to take care of."

"Good to hear that. What is the offer?" replied Mr Mathur.

"We can offer a settlement of 50 lakhs," Ms Siddiqui said.

"That's ridiculous! Don't forget my client is aware of your client's business turnover."

"How much does your client want?"

"My client's demand is for two crores."

"What? Are you joking?"

"My client's life is lonely, loveless, and tough because of Mr Viren. Money does not compensate for the years of abuse and atrocities, but to make a fresh start, Ms Abha wants two crores, including an apartment Mr Viren owns on Noida Expressway," Mr Mathur's voice was calm.

"This is ridiculous! Two crores is too much!" exclaimed Ms Siddiqui.

Viren clenched his fists. He looked as if he would have assaulted Abha if given a chance.

"My client's future is uncertain, while your client is a rich businessman. Two crores is not a large amount for Mr Joon."

"Let me get back to you, though I don't think it is possible. You may wait here while we discuss among ourselves," Ms Siddiqui replied.

Mr Mathur and Abha waited in the conference room. Tea and snacks were served to them. Ms Siddiqui, along with Viren and his cousins, returned 45 minutes later.

"We can offer one crore inclusive of the flat on Noida Expressway," said Ms Siddiqui. Mr Mathur and Abha were aware of how far they could stretch the Joons and turned down the offer.

Finally, after one more round of negotiations with terse exchanges and allegations on each other's clients, they settled the matter—a flat worth about a crore on the Noida Expressway and an additional one crore. Viren sulked and fumed, his cousins swore inaudibly, while Abha maintained a stoic face. However, deep down, both parties were glad that the divorce proceedings would be over on the next date when the lawyers would inform the court about the mutually agreed settlement.

***

"Sir, please come to DM Sir's chamber urgently." Mr Prabhat Ranjan's PA was on the line.

"Can you tell Sir that I am busy with RTI hearings? I will come later," Samar said.

"Let me recheck, Sir," the PA replied hesitantly.

Samar hated leaving proceedings in between and keeping the appellants and respondents waiting.

"Sorry, Sir. DM Sir is saying you must come right away," the PA said in an alarmed voice.

Samar left for the DM's office, irritated.

The DM looked agitated. "Samar, what is this? If I asked for you, it must be urgent."

"Sir, I was in the middle of RTI proceedings," Samar defended himself.

"RTI hearings can wait," he dismissed Samar's explanation. "I suppose you know Mr Radhey Mohan Munjal is a senior retired officer. He called me 10 minutes back, complaining about you."

"Yes, Sir. I know him," Samar said.

"He is a very senior officer, and was powerful during his time. He said you are delaying some simple case." Mr Ranjan gave Samar an annoyed look.

"Sir, let me explain, please. The land in question is Gram Sabha land. The seller, Tyagi, illegally occupied it. Mr Munjal's relative had bought it on Power of Attorney from Tyagi. How can it be mutated in his favour?" Samar explained in a single breath.

"I don't know all that! Mr Munjal is a senior officer, and I don't want him calling me to complain again. If you displease him, be ready to face the music."

A week later, Samar received another call from Mr Munjal.

"Beta, what happened? Why are you not concluding the case? Mr Gupta bought the land, and it should be mutated in his favour.

It's as simple as that!" Mr Munjal said, trying hard to remain calm.

"Sir, please understand. The land is disputed. It is not so simple," Samar replied in a polite tone.

"No, young man, the owner sold the land to Mr Gupta. It is not Mr Gupta's problem if your records are not updated."

"Sir, I verified the old records. The land is Gram Sabha land, and the seller encroached upon it."

"That is not Mr Gupta's fault. If the seller encroached on it, what were you people doing? When I was an SDM, we did not take so much time to decide," Mr Munjal said in an agitated tone.

"Sir, it is public land. It can't be mutated in Mr Gupta's favour," Samar said firmly.

"This is simply harassment. Do you want me to speak to your Divisional Commissioner about you?" Mr Munjal asked, indirectly threatening to complain.

"Sir, I have given you the facts. Sorry to have disappointed you..."

Samar lost the dial tone while speaking. Mr Munjal seemed to have disconnected the call.

***

"Do you still love me?"

The sudden question took Samar by surprise. He had come to meet Abha for coffee at the Janak Puri District Centre after his office hours.

There was a momentary pause. Samar was perplexed by the question. He was married and about to become a father soon.

She repeated, "Do you love me?"

"What is the purpose of such a pointless question?" muttered Samar.

"It is not pointless. I am free from Viren. I need to settle down, and want to have someone in my life," Abha said plainly.

"Hmm.... I don't know."

"You need to think it over, Samar."

Samar glanced around, unsure and confused. Abha seemed determined to extract a reply from him that day.

"Samar, I am a divorcee. I was not fortunate enough to find a suitable life partner. I know you loved me during our civil services preparation days. You had confessed many times to me…"

"But you were busy with Punit Oberoi. You wanted to marry him," retorted Samar.

"That was a different phase." After a pause, she said, "You used to love me. Do you still do?"

"Why is that important?"

"It is important for all of us. It is important to know why you are spending time with me while your wife is expecting your child."

"Because you are a friend, and you need my support."

"I don't need a friend; I need a life partner. I need a lover, Samar. I want a child, and I want you to be the father of my child."

"This is ridiculous! What are you saying?"

"I am serious. I want to have a normal life with a loving partner and a child. Is it wrong to want that in one's life?"

"No… It is not wrong. You are entitled to your happiness."

"Then why are you saying it's ridiculous? Tell me, will you be able to give me these joys of life?"

"I can't understand what you are talking about."

"Why do you keep meeting me, then?" Abha asked.

"I don't know. Maybe because we are friends."

"You mean, you don't love me anymore?" said Abha.

"You don't understand friendship, Abha. You don't even understand me. Not now, not then!" protested Samar, controlling his voice to avoid being overheard by others around him. Abha looked agitated and unsatisfied with his response.

"It's getting late. We had better call it a day," said Samar, as he rose from his seat abruptly. Abha followed him out of the cafe.

"You can avoid answering me, but you need to think about it, Samar. I will wait for your answer," Abha said while parting ways.

Samar got into his Gypsy hurriedly.

"Drive home fast!" he said to the driver.

As the vehicle made its way through rush hour traffic, Samar asked himself whether he loved Abha. He had been meeting her regularly, especially since she took those sleeping pills.

Do I care for Abha because I love her? I am not sure.

If I do, I need to accept it.

Does it mean I don't love Jyotsna? Half an hour later, he reached home and changed his clothes. He was not hungry and settled for a glass of warm milk with a pinch of turmeric powder to help him fall asleep. But the milk did not help, as his mind was restless.

Am I ready to leave Jyotsna and my unborn child for Abha?

Am I confusing empathy and care with love? Is Abha also doing the same?

How did I get into such a situation?

Samar tossed and turned on his bed. Sleep evaded him till the wee hours of the morning.

***

CHAPTER 23

"Sir, Divcom madam's PA is on the line," Ajay, Samar's Reader, said. "May I transfer the line?"

"Yes," Samar replied.

After a beep, he heard the PA's voice on the other side, "Sir, Ma'am wants to speak to you. May I connect?"

"Yes, sure."

There was another beep.

"Hello, Samar. How are you?" Mrs Nalini Sharma asked.

"Good afternoon, Ma'am. I am fine. Thank you," Samar said, anticipating what was coming next. It was uncommon for a Divisional Commissioner to call the SDM rather than the district DM.

"Samar, Mr R. M. Munjal, a senior retired officer, mentioned a revenue case pending in your court. Is it so?"

This was about a week after he had received the call from Mr Munjal.

"Yes, Ma'am. The case is Gram Sabha Rewla Khanpur vs. Harender Gupta."

"What is it about?"

"Ma'am, Mr Gupta, the respondent in this case, had bought the land in question from one Mr Tyagi. Mr Gupta had applied for the mutation, which was done in Mr Gupta's favour by the Tehsildar."

"Oh! I see. Please carry on," Mrs Nalini Sharma replied.

"Ma'am, the land belongs to the Gram Sabha, which has challenged the mutation. The Gram Sabha counsel lodged the case in SDM Kapashera's court."

"Hmm... But Munjal Sir claimed the ownership is in Harender Gupta's name. Did you check the records?" she asked patiently.

"Yes, Ma'am, I have verified the old revenue records. The land belongs to the Gram Sabha."

"Oh, I see! He said something else."

"Ma'am, I have verified the facts myself."

"Okay. I got it. Just submit a report to me on the facts confidentially."

"Definitely, Ma'am. I am sorry, Ma'am, but what Munjal Sir wants is not possible."

"Don't worry. I will handle him. Always follow what is within the rules. I trust you."

Samar was thrilled at hearing these words of appreciation from the Divisional Commissioner. Samar admired her leadership and cool demeanour. She was an understanding, no-nonsense, dynamic, results-oriented officer who protected her officers when they were on the right side of the law. Samar was not worried.

***

Abha had been pondering over her future since the divorce agreement. She was free from Viren, had a good amount of money and a flat on Noida Expressway, where no one knew her. She could restart with a clean slate. But she longed for a special person in her life, someone who would love her. Under the circumstances, Samar was the best bet.

Abha invested a major part of the settlement in mutual funds, fixed deposits, etc. She set aside eight lakhs for her immediate expenses, including shopping for expensive clothes, white goods, and furniture for her flat. She decided to travel to Europe for a vacation in the second week of August. She called Samar. "I am going on a vacation to Europe."

"That's good. You deserve a vacation."

"I was wondering if you could come along. I will sponsor your trip."

"Oh! That's an irresistible offer. However, I can't come, Abha. You know it."

"Why? Why can't you come? Your wife is not even here."

"My wife's pregnancy is in an advanced stage, and I might have to go to Tezpur. Besides, it will be a lot of hassle for a government servant to clear the formalities," said Samar.

"Your wife's due date is on the 14th of September. You can be back by then."

"I can't leave my wife like that. I have responsibilities."

"Your in-laws are with her."

"Hmm…"

"Why bother about your wife if you don't love her? Eventually, you might leave her for me, if you love me," said Abha plainly.

"I do care for you, but I care for my wife, too. I cannot break Jyotsna's trust in me," Samar said in an assertive tone.

"Are you sure she trusts you?" countered Abha.

Samar remained silent, unsure of the answer.

"Samar, I think you love me, so stop beating around the bush."

Samar did not react. He was confused and clueless.

"I want a man in my life, a lover, a partner. I told you to give me a straightforward answer, but you keep avoiding the subject," said Abha firmly.

"Okay. Can you answer one question, Abha?"

"Ask!"

"Do you love me?" Samar asked.

"I don't know if I love you, but I respect you. You are a great human being and a dependable person. You will make a great life partner," responded Abha.

"So, you are not sure if you love me?"

"I don't think I love you at present. Love grows on me, so eventually, I will fall in love. But I know you are a great catch!" Abha carried on.

"Hmm…That's flattering," Samar said.

"Anyway, I shall go on a solitary trip. But when I return, I expect an honest answer from you."

"Hmm…"

"I will wait for your answer. My future will depend on it," Abha concluded.

Samar was unsure about the intensity of his feelings for Jyotsna or whether he even loved her. However, he was certain that he cared for her. He was looking forward to the birth of his child and to their life together, even though he had never explicitly expressed his feelings to Jyotsna.

He was certain he had loved Abha in the past. She had seemed to have some invisible power over him. He empathized with her present condition and wanted her to be happy in life.

But, love...It was too big a word!

***

Abha had a long-cherished desire to tour foreign lands. After a tumultuous and painful period in her life, a vacation in Europe was a dream come true..

Abha took a Schengen visa for six months and kept a loose schedule of the trip. She landed in Paris on a beautiful evening. The exquisite Eiffel Tower, the serenely beautiful Seine River, the quaint cafes, and the grand avenues mesmerized her. The next stop was Madrid, which was lovely, lively, and mysterious. Next, she travelled to Barcelona, after which she flew to Rome, Milan, and then Venice. Her final destination was Vienna in Austria. Abha visited monuments, palaces, museums, famous streets, and riversides, and saw interesting people, travellers, history lovers, lovers, students, and backpackers. She even befriended a few of them. She stayed in all sorts of hotels and motels, visited bars and restaurants, relished local cuisine and wine, and enjoyed the freedom. Abha was living as if there was no tomorrow...

***

Samar was in the middle of a hearing in the Revenue Court proceedings in the third week of August when he received a call from Meghna.

"*Bhindow*! *Bhindow*! Jenny *Ba* is in a lot of pain!" Meghna said breathlessly.

"What happened?"

Samar got up from the court and moved to the anteroom.

"Jenny ba is in pain. We are shifting her to the hospital."

"What happened?"

Samar heard loud voices in the background. Dr Deka was calling out to Meghna.

"*Bhindow*, I have to go now. I will talk to you later."

Meghna disconnected the call. Samar called back, but there was no response. He tried Dr Deka's and Jyotsna's numbers, but neither responded. It was 5:45 pm. He called it a day and redialled

Meghna's number on his way back home. This time, she took his call.

"What is the matter? Why didn't you pick up? Is Jyotsna okay?" Samar threw a volley of questions at Meghna.

"*Bhindow*, Jenny ba had premature labour. We are in the hospital. She is under observation in the ICU," replied Meghna.

"Oh my God! Is Jyotsna all right?"

"She is better now."

"The due date was another two weeks from now. How did the labour pain start so early?" muttered Samar.

"The doctor said that such things happen sometimes in cases of first pregnancy."

"Can I speak to Deuta?"

Meghna passed the phone to Dr Deka.

"Deuta, I had scheduled my ticket for the 10th of September. Should I come earlier?" asked Samar.

"It is up to you. We are here. Delivery can occur on the due date or earlier. Such things can't be predicted," Dr Deka answered.

"Can I speak to Jyotsna now?"

"She is sleeping. Let her rest for a while. I will call you later once she wakes up."

Samar finished his dinner and lay down for a while, waiting for the call. He dozed off and was startled awake late in the night by the ringtone of his mobile. It was Jyotsna.

"Hello! I was waiting for your call," said Samar, getting up from the bed.

"Hello, I was asleep when you called. I had labour pain today." Her voice was weak.

"Yes, Meghna told. Are you fine now?"

"Yes, I think so… I wish you were here by my side."

"Don't worry. I am coming on the 10th of September."

"Can you prepone it? I have a feeling I might have a premature delivery."

"I was planning to take my paternity leave once my ELs expire. But let me see."

"I am scared. I don't know what will happen. I hope our baby is fine," Jyotsna said worriedly.

"Don't worry. I understand your state of mind. Okay, I will come as early as possible."

"Samar, I have been having recurrent bad dreams about the safety of our baby. I feel drained, weak, and exhausted all the time."

"Don't stress yourself with negative thoughts. Now, you need to relax and rest. It's very late in the night."

"Yes, sure. You also have office tomorrow. Good night."

"Good night."

***

CHAPTER 24

After the labour pain subsided, Jyotsna was fine for two days. On the third day, her water broke, and the doctor kept her under observation for the next 24 hours. It was the thirty-sixth week. In medical terms, Jyotsna had PROM, or pre-labour rupture of membranes.

Earlier, Samar had preponed his visit to the 31st of August, but when her water broke on the 25th, he rushed to catch the earliest available flight the next morning. He was restless, worried, and continuously taking updates on her condition.

"Meghna, I have just landed in Guwahati. Hope everything is fine?" he asked.

"The doctor has been trying to induce labour pain since morning, *Bhindow,* but labour is not getting induced," Meghna said, her voice tense. "She said she will try again. I will update you."

Outside Borjhar airport, several taxi drivers approached Samar, asking, *"Kahan jana hai,* Dada?"

"Tezpur."

"No, Dada, we will not go to Tezpur," they replied.

Samar approached several taxi drivers, but all of them refused. A *bandh* had been called by a local students' association, and the drivers feared any taxi plying that side would be pelted with stones. Finally, Samar had to take a taxi up to Khanapara.

He reached Khanapara around 12:30 pm. Again, at the Khanapara stand, most taxis refused to travel to Tezpur. The bandh culture had taken deep roots in the Northeast, and people avoided any sort of trouble with the bandh callers.

"Kahan jaataa hai, Babu?" a local Assamese driver asked.

"Tezpur," Samar said.

"There is a bandh on that side. It's not safe."

"I know, but I need to be there on time, please."

The driver seemed reluctant. Samar offered to pay Rs 150 more than the usual fare. The driver agreed.

Once inside the taxi, Samar called Meghna. "I have boarded a taxi now. What is the situation?"

"Oh! What took you so long to get a taxi, *Bhindow*?" Meghna asked.

"There is a bandh, and all taxis refused to travel to Tezpur. I managed a taxi from Khanapara. I am passing through Jorabaat."

"Oh, I see! I heard about the bandh. The doctor has planned for a C-section." Meghna continued, "Please be careful on the way."

"I will. Keep me updated."

"Dada, *apuni Asomiya neki?"* the curious driver inquired in Assamese. ("Are you Assamese?)

"Yes," answered Samar.

"Apuni ki kore?" (What do you do?)

"Moi Delhitt Officer hoi! Tezpurot mur wifor ghar." (I am an officer in Delhi. I am visiting my wife's home.)

"Bhal lagise, bor bhal lagise! Amar Asomiya officer bahut kom." (It feels great to see a rare Assamese officer.)

"Mur naam tu Prince Barua, Dada. *Naam tu hai prince, prince nohoi kintu,* Dada," the driver chuckled cheekily. (My name is Prince Barua, brother. But I am not a prince otherwise.)

On the way, Prince Barua narrated his story. He hailed from Kaliabor town and had bought a taxi on loan. He had a wife, two young children, parents, and three younger brothers to feed.

After a while, Samar dozed off in the back seat. At around 1:30 pm, he stopped at a dhaba for a quick lunch. Meanwhile, Meghna informed him that the gynaecologist would perform a C-section in an hour.

After about two hours, trucks, buses, and private cars started plying on the National Highway. By the time they reached Kuhimari, a small town, there was heavy traffic, which moved at a snail's pace. On being asked, an onlooker told Samar that the bandh callers had squatted on the Kaliabhomora bridge till around 2:00 pm, after which local police intervened and removed the protestors. A few stone-pelting incidents at passing vehicles near Dolapani and Hatibandha were reported. The slow traffic was the after-effect of the blockade for nearly three hours. Meanwhile, Jyotsna's C-section operation had commenced.

It took Samar about six hours to reach Tezpur from the airport.

Prince Barua dropped him at the Sunrise Maternity Hospital.

The C-section was successful, and Jyotsna was fine, though weak. She gave birth to a baby girl weighing two kg. They kept the baby in the NICU.

"Come, Samar. Jyotsna is exhausted, but fine," Dr Deka said.

"I got delayed on the way," Samar replied.

"Samar, I am afraid the baby has a breathing problem and jaundice."

"Oh!" The baby's health issue dampened his spirits. "I want to see them," Samar said anxiously.

"You can see Jyotsna in a while. However, the NICU has specific visiting hours. The next time is 10 am tomorrow."

Samar went downstairs to the hospital canteen with Meghna for a cup of coffee.

"Jenny ba was terrified before the operation. She scared us to death," Meghna disclosed.

"I wish I could have reached before the operation. But these bandhs!" Samar said regretfully.

"I know. Anyway, meet Jenny ba, and then the driver will drive you back home."

"I will wait here until tomorrow. I will come back after freshening up."

"No, no, *Bhindow*! You need to rest after a long day. Maa and I will stay with Jenny ba tonight."

***

Jyotsna's eyes glistened with tears upon seeing Samar.

"No.. No… Don't get up," he said.

Samar walked to her bed and held her hands. He sat down beside her on the bed.

"I am happy you made it, finally, Daddy," Jyotsna said.

"I am relieved. Thank God, you are fine," Samar said.

"Our baby cannot breathe properly, Samar…" Jyotsna's tears flowed freely. "Why is God punishing such an innocent soul?"

"Don't think so much. You had a major operation. You need to rest," Samar comforted her.

"I used to have bad dreams…." Jyotsna mumbled in a low, dejected voice.

"Have faith in God. Everything will be fine." He put up a brave front.

Later, Samar and Dr Deka headed home. After a warm bath and an early dinner, Samar retired to bed on Dr Deka's advice.

"You need to be energized for the coming days. Jyotsna will be in the ICU for another three or four days, depending on her recovery. We don't know when the baby will recover," Dr Deka said.

Samar woke up early and got ready to visit the hospital. He had spent a restless night.

Around 11 am, Samar visited the NICU. The room had a few cradle beds where newborns were laid. Samar's eyes scanned the room, looking for the cradle bed number eight, where his baby lay. The child looked tiny, pale, and weak. He recalled that Abhimanyu did not look so small when he first saw him after his birth. They had focused white light on the baby's skin, which had a yellowish tinge.

"Is she all right?" Samar asked.

"She will be fine, Sir. This setup is to treat the jaundice," the nurse who was standing at the entrance informed him.

The baby had an oxygen hood affixed over her nose to support her breathing. She was breathing with some effort. He stared at her for a long time. Tears rolled down his cheeks.

Why is God punishing such an innocent soul? Am I somehow responsible for it?

Samar stayed overnight at the hospital for the next two days. Paediatricians regularly monitored the child. The breathing problem persisted, and the child needed to be kept under observation.

Jyotsna recovered in the next three days and was ready for discharge. The baby's condition improved as the newborn's jaundice disappeared. However, the breathing problem remained. Although the family hesitated to leave the child at the NICU in the hospital, they had no choice as the hospital discharged Jyotsna on the fourth day after the operation.

***

On the 1st of September, Abha returned to Delhi from Vienna. She dialled Samar's mobile.

"Hey, Samar! It's nice to hear your voice after such a long time," Abha said flirtatiously.

"Accha! Is that so?"

"Yes."

"How is your trip? Are you still in Europe?" Samar responded.

"I am back in Delhi. I had a great time. I met interesting people, experienced different cultures, relished exotic cuisines…"

"I am glad. Which places did you visit?" Samar interrupted.

"Paris, Madrid, Barcelona, Milan, Venice, Rome, Vienna… such exquisitely beautiful places! It was wonderful!"

Abha continued talking about her trip for about five minutes. Samar listened patiently.

"Enough about me. How have you been? Where are you?" Abha asked.

"I am in Tezpur. Jyotsna had a premature delivery. My daughter is having breathing issues," Samar replied.

"Oh! I am so sorry to hear that. Why didn't you tell me before? I went on and on about my trip."

"It's okay. How would you know what I am going through?"

"Still, you should have told me at the beginning."

Samar told her that the baby was pre-term, which had caused such complications.

"Such a poor little soul. This is so unfair," Abha said.

"We can only wait and hope for her recovery."

"Have faith in God. Everything will be fine. I hope Jyotsna is fine."

"She is okay, but worried like me. I am trying to keep my faith intact."

***

The baby gradually showed signs of improvement from the seventh day onward. After another four days, her breathing conditions normalized. The paediatrician gave permission to take her home. Samar had almost lived in the hospital for the entire duration that the baby had been in the NICU.

The arrival of the newborn lifted the spirits in the Deka household. Changing diapers, washing and disinfecting her clothing, bathing and feeding her kept the new parents and the Dekas engaged and animated. They hired a maid for the baby. Jyotsna's recovery was also on track. Samar's 15 days of leave passed rather quickly, and he left for Delhi.

***

CHAPTER 25

A formidable backlog of files greeted Samar. He had to spend long hours at the office for two weeks to restore normalcy.

Back at Tezpur, Jyotsna was gradually picking up the nuances of motherhood. Her mother guided her. Although Jyotsna breastfed the baby, the underweight infant did not show significant weight gain in subsequent weeks. The paediatrician prescribed weight-enhancing milk powder.

Jyotsna barely got time to speak to Samar, and when she did, it was for short intervals. She was always exhausted.

Samar maintained regular contact with her family, excited about his new role as a father. On alternate evenings, he Skyped to see his daughter. They had not decided on a formal name for the child and had addressed her as '*Mainajoni*', an Assamese word for a little girl.

***

The Europe trip had a profound influence on Abha, leading to a major shift in her outlook on life. It was an eye-opener to see how people lead happy, carefree lives, living every moment king-size. She wanted to do the same.

After returning, she did not resume teaching at the school but extended her break. She relished the carefree, leisurely days without having to worry about waking up early to take the school bus, teaching for long hours, returning home exhausted, and cooking afterwards. She lounged around in bed until late. She shopped, visited salons, and enjoyed coffee at popular joints and solitary dinners at fancy restaurants and resto-bars. After acquiring a taste for wine, especially Spanish white wines, she ordered expensive wine at restaurants or stocked it at home. She did not want to return to the usual grind of her earlier, mundane life. Not yet…

A month later, Abha met Samar for coffee. She looked younger, prettier, and lissome, dressed in an aqua-blue tube top and a sleek, long, midnight-blue skirt.

"You look different, slim and sharp," Samar remarked.

"Oh, really! You're joking."

"No. I am serious. You look beautiful, relaxed, and fresh. Just like the Abha of Rajendra Nagar times…"

"*Aha*! Rajendra Nagar times! What else are you reminded of?" Abha teased.

Samar blushed.

"I joined a gym about a fortnight back," Abha smiled, cheeks flushed.

"That must have worked. I can feel the positive aura around you."

"Stop flirting, old man! Don't forget, you are a daddy now," chided Abha.

"Right," Samar sighed.

The waiter came to take their order.

"One chamomile green tea. What will you have?" Abha asked.

Seeing Samar hesitate, she said, "Make it two chamomile green teas and some slices of chocolate mousse cake."

The waiter politely bowed, his eyes lingering for a moment on Abha, and left.

"As always, you ordered for me," Samar observed.

"Don't blame me. I did ask you, but you looked dazed."

"It's okay. You take me for granted always."

"Oh! Sorry. It never occurred to me. Maybe you are right. Usually, I order whenever we are in a restaurant."

"I prefer the same thing when we are together."

"Together!"

Samar flushed when Abha repeated the word meaningfully.

"How is the baby girl and the mother doing?" Abha asked.

"The baby is still underweight. She is keeping Jyotsna busy, who has no time to talk to me these days. My baby is the best thing that has happened to me!" he gushed, his eyes bright.

"So, Mommy is immersed in motherhood. That's why Daddy dear is swimming wayward."

Samar looked uncomfortable. "And why do you look different? Is it the after-effect of the exotic trip or something else?" he asked, changing the topic.

"Can you guess?"

"Did you find a special person?" Samar said.

"Yes."

"Oh!... I mean, great!" Samar pretended to look happy, though he felt a strange tug at his heart.

"*Hahaha*! I was joking." Abha grinned and continued, "Maybe it is the phase I am in. I am free from Viren and family pressures. Probably for the first time, I am the centre of my own life, not some brother, some husband..." She paused, then added, "My trip was liberating. Everywhere I went, I found that people savoured every moment and valued whatever they had."

The waiter served the beverages.

Samar gazed at her, confused, as she sipped her tea, looking out the window. After a short pause, she continued, "Here, in India, we spend a lot of time and energy trying to please others, to prove ourselves to our families and others, to fit ourselves in society's ambit..." Abha sighed, "And in these pursuits, we lose ourselves, worrying about failures and disappointments, we stress ourselves, curse ourselves, punish ourselves, suffer at the hands of others, endure a lot of pain... Why?"

She seemed like a different person to Samar.

Abha took a deep breath and said, "I mean, why should we care? Why should we bother about society? Society does not support us when we are down and lonely."

"You are getting philosophical, but you are right," Samar replied.

"I am going to change my life. I am going to live it my way. Only my way!" Abha said loudly enough to startle the couple at the next table. She seemed oblivious to her surroundings.

"Do you know, Samar, why I wanted to try for the civil services? My father and brother did not want me to study further. So, I considered the civil services as an option to escape their hegemony."

Samar nodded understandingly as she continued her monologue.

"But I got distracted during my preparations. Perhaps I was not fully into it and just wanted to prove my worth to my family.

Maybe that is why I failed. I was drawn to Punit as he introduced me to another world. I saw how girls in big cities enjoyed their freedom. I aspired for their lifestyle and independence. I thought Punit could be the means to achieve all that. That is why I wanted to marry him." She sighed and added, "I don't regret my decision to be involved with him, but destiny had other plans."

"Shall I carry on, or are you bored?" Abha paused to ask Samar.

"Carry on, Madam!"

"So, leaving aside the circumstances in which I married Viren, perhaps I did not invest my emotions in the marriage. That's why it failed."

Samar listened to her, confused and enamoured.

"I was looking for love and support when I met you after so many years. I thought, who would be a better person than you? You loved me, cared for me, empathized with me… I thought you were the best bet for a life companion," Abha paused, then continued, "But I was wrong. Why do I need a life partner?" She took a deep breath. "I just need myself to be happy. No one else can make me happy except myself…"

Samar was puzzled. A few weeks back, Abha had been cajoling him to come back into her life…

How did this sudden change in attitude happen? What does she want?

She seemed different because she was different inside, also.

She declined the offer for dinner. She wanted to get back home to read a classic novel—*Gone with the Wind!*

She never enjoyed reading earlier.

When they parted, Abha handed him a bag. "Here, this is for you."

The bag held two bottles of exotic white wine.

"Thank you."

Abha seemed like a complete stranger with her new perspective. The resentment against others who had traumatized her had vanished. She looked forward to her independent life.

Samar felt disconnected from Abha. He longed to connect with Jyotsna and the baby after the unexpected evening. He called her on the way back home.

"Hey, wifey, how was your day?" Samar asked.

"Very busy… You know, Mainajoni did a new thing today," gushed Jyotsna.

"Let me guess, she called you Mamma!" Samar joked.

"No, she called for her Papa!" Jyotsna said.

"Oh, really? That's fast learning in a month."

"Very funny! She smiled at me for the first time. She already follows me around the room with her eyes. The paediatrician told me babies recognize their mother and smile only after two to three months." Jyotsna was enthused, and so was Samar.

"That's great! She seems to be a fast learner. I am missing these moments."

"You are right, Daddy." She sighed. "I am exhausted again. She wakes up in the night if we switch off the lights. I have to keep the lamp on till she sleeps again."

"She fears darkness, then."

"Yes, I think so. I am sleep-deprived, though."

"Then, sleep for a while during the day," Samar suggested.

"Yes, I do. I leave her with Maa during the morning after feeding her, but I don't sleep soundly during the daytime." Jyotsna yawned. "How was your day?"

"Hectic. I had to finalize two court-related replies connected to some encroachment drive." Samar sighed.

"You mean, boring stuff! Anyway, I am planning to retire early tonight. Mainajoni will wake me up late at night."

"Good luck with that!"

"Good night, Hubby."

***

"I am thinking of booking my ticket for the first week of January and our return tickets for the 20th of January. What do you think?" Samar asked. He was keen to finalize the date for Jyotsna's return to Delhi with the baby.

"Can you wait for a day or two? I will ask Deuta and Maa whether it is safe for a four-month-old baby to travel by flight," Jyotsna said.

"Why do you have to consult them for every decision? You

should listen to your husband as well." Samar was a bit irritated.

"Don't start that again, Samar. I am too tired to argue. I don't know how I would have looked after *Maina* without Deuta, Maa, and Meghna," Jyotsna reasoned.

"You have only one *raag* to sing every time."

Samar's words irritated her, and she lost her temper.

"Where is your family? Your *Nabau* just visited once. After that, there has not been even a single call from them," Jyotsna retorted.

She was right. Amar and Maloti had hardly been in touch with them after Samar's marriage. Maloti harboured a grudge against Jyotsna as both brothers had rejected her sister's proposal for Samar. Samar called them up occasionally for Abhimanyu's sake and sometimes provided funds for his studies.

Sensing his mood, Jyotsna said, "I only said I would ask my parents. Maybe if everything looks good, we can still return to Delhi by the end of January. After all, I need to restart my work as well."

Samar brooded over their disagreements.

How will I live the rest of my life with her?

No, you cannot think like this. You have a baby now. Think about her future. Life is never perfect. It is about compromises and adjustments.

But why should I be the only one to compromise? She needs to understand me, too.

Samar fought a battle within…

***

Samar received a call from Abha a fortnight after their last meeting.

"How was the wine? Did you like it?" Abha asked.

"Did you call me to ask that?" Samar answered.

"Haha!"

"It was delicious. I loved it. You have picked up good taste," Samar said.

"I am glad you liked it. I loved the variety of wine in Europe."

"It seems Europe's fever is still on!"

Abha chuckled. “My Europe trip was an eye-opener for me.”

“Indeed!”

“Samar, I have decided on something serious. Are you free to meet tonight? I wanted to discuss it with you.”

“I will be free after an hour.”

“Great. Just text me a place and time to meet.”

***

CHAPTER 26

Samar arrived half an hour late. Abha was already sitting at a table reserved for them, reading a book.

"Sorry to have kept you waiting. My DC summoned a quick meeting on short notice." Samar was apologetic.

"No problem. In fact, I got a good headstart to select an exotic wine from the vineyards of Argentina and some food." Abha raised her glass of wine.

"I can see that!"

The waiter poured him a glass of wine.

Hungry after a long day, Samar gulped down a spoonful of pasta and ate some feta cheese.

"Wonderful!" Abha had clearly developed a taste for exotic food.

"Now, what did you want to discuss?" asked Samar.

"I am thinking of settling down in Noida."

Samar gave her an incredulous look.

"Don't look so bewildered," she said. "I own a flat there. It was to happen some day."

"What about your school job in Delhi? Aren't you settled in Rajouri?"

"I haven't rejoined the school. The rented house is too small to accommodate all the furniture I ordered."

"That's just an excuse."

Abha barely heard what Samar mumbled.

"I have to start afresh, a life away from known people. The sooner, the better." Abha spoke with finality.

Noida would be far away. Too far away!

Samar felt a tug in his heart.

"How will you stay there all alone? Do you know anyone there? Your flat is on the Noida Expressway. The area is not fully developed. It's not safe to live alone."

"I am aware, but I will manage." After a pause, she continued, "I have thought a lot... I don't need a life partner or a lover. I am done with that!"

"That's new. A few weeks back, you were whining for one."

"Well, things have changed. As I said, this trip was an eye-opener. I was able to enjoy it solo. Besides, I won't be alone."

"What do you mean?" Samar asked.

"I wanted your help. Do you remember you told me about an orphaned child, a girl you rescued in a raid?"

"Yes."

"Where is she now? What was her name?"

"Roshni. Why are you asking?"

"Yes, Roshni… I want to adopt her."

"What? Are you serious?"

"I am really serious. Will you help me? I don't know the adoption procedure."

"Last I heard, the Child Welfare Committee could not trace any living relatives, so it ordered that Roshni be kept in a children's shelter home until she is rehabilitated."

"Is it possible to adopt her?"

"I think so. She does not have living parents. Adoption is one way to rehabilitate her."

"Will you help me?" Abha took hold of his hand.

"Are you really serious?"

"Do you think I am joking, talking about shifting to Noida and adopting a child? Of course, I am serious."

"Okay. We will have to present your case for adoption. I hope they will agree, though it might be tough."

"Why will it be tough?" Abha asked.

Samar hesitated, then said, "Because you are a single parent."

Abha looked disappointed. "That's not fair. Very few people come forward to adopt in India. Adoption rules should be relaxed."

"Don't worry. I will recommend your case."

"That would be great. I am glad you understand," Abha said softly.

"Come on, Abha. You are a friend."

After a pause, he asked, "But why Roshni?"

"Being a girl, I was not allowed to make independent decisions about my own life. I want Roshni to have an independent life. I will give her freedom, care, and love, send her to the best school, best college… I will fulfil all her needs, give her everything I never had."

"Hmm… I got it. You have my support. I will request my DC to speak to CWC members."

"Thank you." Abha folded her hands.

"Don't be so formal."

Abha relaxed. "I have something more to say."

She paused, then said, "I have decided to start life afresh with Roshni, or if not her, another adopted girl child. It's time you settled down, too."

"I am settled. What do you mean?" Samar asked, looking surprised.

"Are you? Are you mentally settled, Samar?"

Abha squeezed his hand and continued, "You are not settled. Not yet. You are only married to Jyotsna, not settled with her."

He felt uncomfortable.

"Samar, you have a child now. You must decide whether you love Jyotsna. You can't stand in two boats."

Samar maintained a stoic silence.

"Before I left for Europe, I was pestering you to choose me. I found you unsure and non-committal. I thought you were torn between me and your duty and responsibility towards Jyotsna. I pondered a lot, and now it is clear to me that you used to love me back then, but not anymore."

Abha took a long breath and continued.

"Although you care for Jyotsna, you think you don't love her. But I think somewhere deep down, you love her. You have kept your feelings in check, which prevents you from loving her all the way. You are being cautious and non-committal toward Jyotsna, since you were hurt by your first love. That is because of me…"

Abha paused.

Samar admitted in a sad tone, "Yes, you have hurt me a lot in the past."

"I know that, and I am very sorry. Few people are fortunate enough to get another chance at love. Jyotsna loves you, and naturally, she has expectations from you. You hold yourself back, she gets disappointed and exasperated… Learn to love her back and express your feelings explicitly. Let go of the past."

"You are talking strangely. It seems like the wine has got to you!"

"I am completely in my senses. Otherwise, tell me, do you love me?"

Samar pondered but could not say yes.

"See? You don't love me. You care for me as a friend. Don't mess up your life. Go back to Jyotsna and settle down. And to aid you in that, I promise, I will go out of your life."

Samar felt as if someone had punched him hard.

"How will you settle down, Abha? It is a long life ahead."

"I will have Roshni with me."

Abha poured some more wine into her empty glass.

"Don't change the subject. You need to clear the cobwebs that have gathered over the years. You need to admit to yourself that you no longer love me. You need to open your heart to Jyotsna. Soon, you will realize you love her."

"I am confused. I don't understand a few things about Jyotsna."

"Like what?"

"Every time I try to get close to her, I fail. She has too many high expectations of me. I get overwhelmed by them and her list of dos and don'ts of the perfect life she has in her mind."

"Did she have a boyfriend or lover before you?"

"I don't think so. Her family was her lifeline. It still is!"

"Then, in that case, you are her Prince Charming!" Abha said. "Every girl has a certain predetermined image of a lover or husband. Since she did not have any love relationship before you, naturally, she will want you to fit into that image."

Samar said nothing.

"It is normal for any woman to have expectations from her husband. You need to realize one thing. She did not come with any baggage, like you or me. She came with a simple motive—to love you and be loved back. She deserves your love, attention, and indulgence."

"You say it as if it is so simple!"

"It is simple. Just free your emotions and go with the flow."

"Are you planning to be a counsellor?"

"Don't be sarcastic. Fix your relationship before it's too late. Also, you have a daughter now. Don't you love her?"

"I do." Samar's eyes lit up at the mention of his daughter.

"Then, that settles it. Sort your life, Samar. Trust me, it is important."

***

A week later, Samar booked a flight to Guwahati. He kept his trip a surprise for Jyotsna, though Meghna and the Dekas were aware of it. It was not in his nature to be impulsive. Perhaps, he needed a break, needed to see his daughter, and needed to be with someone… now that Abha seemed to have exited his life.

During his flight, Samar thought about Jyotsna. After their marriage, tender shoots of love had sprouted. But their love had not been enough to fill the void left by Abha. Perhaps Samar had restrained his emotions, regulated his love, and the void was too profound, too expansive to be filled.

He had landed in Delhi a few years back as a gullible, raw IAS aspirant, pursuing his aspirations. There were financial constraints and pressure to crack the exam. Abha had appeared in his life. He had tried to restrain his feelings, but he still fell for her. However, circumstances and situations eventually led to Abha's exit from his life. Her unforeseen exit left a deep void. Perhaps the time had come to fill that void.

***

CHAPTER 27

The doorbell at the Dekas' rang. Jyotsna had ordered diapers from the local chemist's shop and opened the door, expecting the delivery boy. Samar was at the door. For a brief moment, she was taken aback, not sure whether it was reality or an illusion of her mind.

"Hi."

Jyotsna stood there stunned. Samar stepped in and hugged her tightly. She lightly put her arms around him.

"How are you here? Come inside."

They disengaged themselves and walked into the living room, hand in hand.

"Where is Mainajoni?" Samar asked softly.

"I just put her to bed. It's a struggle to make her sleep. She is such an overactive baby!" Jyotsna answered.

"You look haggard." Samar patted her head.

"Yes, she keeps me busy. Your daughter wakes up several times in the night." Jyotsna sighed. "Why didn't you tell me you were coming?"

"I just took off. I missed both of you."

"Now, I am more surprised."

"No. I really mean it."

"Okay, Daddy." Jyotsna punched him lightly in the stomach and said, "It seems you have been missing your workouts. I can see a paunch."

"Yes, I have been eating at odd hours and missing workouts due to work pressure."

"Anyway, you freshen up. Let me switch on the geyser."

The Deka family joined them. They pretended to be surprised at his sudden arrival. They exchanged greetings as Jyotsna dragged his suitcase to the guest room.

The warm shower was refreshing. Samar changed into fresh clothes.

Oh, my little angel! I will always love and protect you!

Samar made a silent promise as he gazed at his two-and-a-half-month-old baby asleep in the bedroom. She looked contented and calm. His eyes moistened.

After a light dinner, Samar held his daughter in his arms as he talked to her. She looked at him with inquisitive eyes. A while later, Jyotsna came in and said, "It's time for her feeding. You must be tired. Why don't you rest now?"

"I need to talk to you. Come back once Mainajoni is asleep."

About an hour later, Jyotsna came to check on Samar. He had dozed off, tired from a long day. She switched off the light and left.

***

Samar woke up late the next morning. After he had bathed, the maid brought breakfast for him. Jyotsna was nowhere to be seen.

When the maid came back to clear the table, she told him Jyotsna had gone to the market, while the baby was getting massaged.

Samar settled down to read a book and dozed off on the lounge chair itself. He was awoken only much later by the sounds of lunch being laid on the table.

Shortly after, the maid came to call him for lunch. "Bhindow, your lunch is laid. Please call me if you need anything."

"Has your Baidow come back?" he inquired.

"No, Bhindow. Baidow has instructed me to serve you lunch. She will be late."

The lunch was elaborate. The spread of delicacies teased his taste buds, and Samar ate till he was full. The heavy, sumptuous lunch called for an afternoon siesta.

Jyotsna came around 4:30 pm to wake him up for the evening tea.

"Where were you all day?"

"I went shopping for baby milk supplements and other stuff. Enjoy your tea and snacks. I will come back later."

After tea, he strolled around the town. He bought some pastries from a bakery, a few baby outfits made of soft hosiery material, a pair of baby towels, a baby wrap, and a hamper of baby skincare products.

"Oh, Daddy! Your daughter missed you," Jyotsna said when he came back.

"Let me wash my hands. Bring her to me."

Jyotsna handed him the baby.

"You both enjoy each other's company. I have to go." Jyotsna left while Samar played with the baby. He sat with her for some time, then he sauntered around the room. After half an hour, he placed her on the bed and rubbed his nose on her tummy. Mainajoni giggled.

After another delicious dinner, he waited for Jyotsna eagerly, passing the time with the book he had tried to read the previous night.

Jyotsna appeared after about an hour.

"What took you so long?"

"She just slept. I am exhausted."

"Revive yourself, Wifey. We need a long discussion."

"What is it? Can't it wait till tomorrow?"

"No, I need to confess something important." Samar looked serious. Jyotsna sighed and sat down beside him on the bed.

"Is it about Abha?" Jyotsna asked evenly.

"Yes, and No. It is about all of us."

Jyotsna's heart raced, but she managed to maintain a brave, nonchalant countenance.

Samar spoke slowly and softly. "I knew Abha before I met you. We were both preparing for the Civil Services Examination in Delhi." He paused, trying to read Jyotsna's eyes, but failed.

"I guess you think something is going on between me and Abha."

Jyotsna avoided his eyes.

Is he going to confess to the affair between them?

"You won't say anything, but I know you have some suspicion," Samar said.

Jyotsna remained silent.

"During our preparation, we became friends, and we got close. I think I fell in love with her," Samar said in a hesitant tone.

He looked into Jyotsna's eyes, expecting a strong reaction from her. He was confused by her nonchalant attitude. She looked unaffected, but her heart ached.

"I won't deny that I loved and cared for her. We used to go to classes together, study together, meet often, and go out. It lasted for several months. Then, she ditched me. Actually, I think she never loved me. It was only me who loved her."

He reached for her hand. She slowly withdrew her hand from his grip.

"Later, she started going out with another fellow, Punit. During that time, we fell apart. I immersed myself in studies, but it was a painful, dreadful time for me, struggling with the pressure of clearing the exam and mending my broken heart."

He must have loved her dearly. The heartache still seems fresh!

"During that time, she wanted to marry Punit, but he refused. After that, she reconnected with me."

Jyotsna's continued silence made him nervous.

"It was my second attempt. I was to write my Mains. She failed to clear her Prelims for the second time. Her family was coercing her to get married. One day, she came to me, pleading that her brother was coming to take her away. She asked me for help running away from Delhi. We ran away to Chandigarh."

"Oh, my God! You even eloped with her!" Jyotsna was shocked and finally broke her silence.

"No, we did not elope as a couple. I was helping her run away. We did not think… we were very young then. It was an impulsive decision without contemplating the consequences."

"Did she ditch you again after Chandigarh?"

"Nothing of that sort." Samar laughed lightly. "The next day, her brother and his goons found out the address of the hideout and came to Chandigarh. They beat me black and blue and took her away."

"Oh!"

"I was unconscious for several hours. Sunny, the IPS friend you met once, admitted me to PGI. I suffered serious fractures and had to miss my Mains."

"And what happened to Abha?"

"Her family married her off to a rich businessman."

"Oh! That's shocking!"

"I had no contact with her after they whisked her away that morning. Thereafter, I cleared my exams the next year and joined the service. And, the rest you know," Samar concluded.

"That's it?" asked Jyotsna.

"Yes."

"You are still not being truthful with me, Samar," Jyotsna said grimly.

"I have told you everything truthfully. I loved Abha in the past, but I don't love her anymore. She is a friend, that is all. That's the whole truth, believe me."

"I don't believe you. I know she was in regular touch with you when I was here," Jyotsna said quietly.

"Abha contacted me suddenly one day while you were here. She narrated about her forced marriage to Viren Joon. Unfortunately, it did not work out, and she filed for a divorce. She needed emotional support. As a friend, I rendered that. But it was nothing more than that. I swear!" Samar explained.

"What about that phone call I accidentally picked up?"

"That day when she called on my mobile, she was in a low mood. After she could not speak to me, she tried to commit suicide. That is why I was angry with you for not telling me about her call."

Jyotsna stared at the wall, conflicted.

Samar continued, "Abha is from a conservative family. Her family made all the decisions, be it about her studies, her groom, or the number of attempts for the civil services exam."

He paused, then said, "She was undergoing painful divorce proceedings in court involving allegations, counter-allegations, character assassination… she suffered a lot. Please try to understand the situation."

"You care for her, I get it. You expect me to understand your relationship with her, but what about my feelings? What about your care, support, and responsibilities towards me?"

Samar lamented regretfully, "I tried my best to make you happy, but maybe it was not enough. I gave Abha too much priority. You must have felt neglected. I am sorry. I did not understand that you had expectations of me. I admit it was my mistake."

Jyotsna looked at the wall clock. She was tired, physically and emotionally.

"I assure you, the Abha phase is over. In fact, it was over long ago. I failed to realize that Abha's reappearance could create ripples in our married life," Samar admitted.

His eyes filled with tears as he pleaded with her. Jyotsna looked away as tears came into her eyes, too.

Samar reached for her hand, squeezed it lightly, and said, "The reality is, I don't love Abha, I love you!"

"I don't think so…" Jyotsna retorted instantly and withdrew her hand again.

"I do… I love you. I have realized it gradually."

"Please don't play with my emotions again. Please!"

"Jyotsna, how do I make you believe me? I will break off all ties with Abha. But please trust me. I was a fool. I did not know how to express my feelings to you."

"You have broken my heart. You have hurt my feelings terribly." Jyotsna's voice was choked with pent-up emotions. She cleared her throat and said, "I don't have any past. You are the first man in my life."

"So, when I met you, you thought I was your Prince Charming!"

Samar tried to lighten the mood and succeeded in bringing a smile to her face.

"Something like that. I fell in love with you," Jyotsna admitted shyly. "I thought you would love me, care for me, give me everything. I thought I would fulfil all my girlish wishes and desires, and we would live happily ever after."

"But I disappointed you, hurt you…" Samar said. The tears streamed down his cheeks.

Jyotsna became quiet again.

"What do I say now?" Samar asked.

"I believe what you said about Abha, but I have wounds that will take time to heal…"

Wiping off his tears, Samar said, "Don't say that, Jyotsna! I love and miss both of you. Come to Delhi. I came to take you both home."

"Samar, maybe you don't love Abha anymore, but her spell has cast its shadow on our relationship."

"Jyotsna, please forgive me. Please… Please understand!"

It was almost midnight. They were speaking in hushed tones to avoid being overheard.

"Samar, it is very late now. Go to sleep. We will talk again tomorrow."

As she got up abruptly, Samar pulled her back on his lap. He kissed her forehead. "Leave me, Samar," Jyotsna protested half-heartedly.

He kissed her on the lips. She trembled at his touch..

***

"Let's take some time off. Let us leave everything to time."

Those were Jyotsna's parting lines the night before. The discussion had been inconclusive. Jyotsna did not relent at his pleadings. Rather, she was distraught. Her fears that Abha was more than a friend were confirmed. She was overwhelmed with fear and apprehension about their future together.

Will Samar emerge from Abha's spell?

Will Abha always overshadow our relationship?

Jyotsna avoided Samar all day. He was restive and spent most of the day playing with and cuddling his baby girl. The baby seemed to be recognizing him gradually.

After dinner, he waited for Jyotsna. She came in after a while.

"What is your decision? Will you come home with me this time?" Samar asked. He failed to evoke any response.

"I know I have hurt you. You are still angry. But I assure you I did nothing wrong."

"I hope so," Jyotsna said.

"I did not cultivate our relationship properly. That is where I failed." Samar cleared his throat and continued, "However, the onus was also on you to correct me, so I could know my shortcomings and rectify them. I'm sorry to say this, but you didn't correct me either." He had practised these lines all day. He knew it was risky, but he had no choice.

"I need time to think," Jyotsna said.

"Let's start afresh. Let our daughter be the harbinger of our new beginning."

"It is not that simple, Samar. Things can't become normal overnight. At this stage, I want to devote my energy to my daughter."

"The basic point is I have realized I care for you and want you in my life, nobody else. Forgive me for the sake of our future and our baby," Samar pleaded.

"It takes time to heal wounds. I urge you not to pressurize me more than I can take. Let things move at their natural pace," Jyotsna replied.

"Don't be so harsh on me."

"As long as you are here, don't say anything on this subject. I hate it when I can't control my tears," she said in a choked voice.

Samar did not push further. He was not sure of what to say more or how to convince her.

***

Samar stayed for six more days. In between, he visited his brother's family in Guwahati. Abhimanyu was now a handsome teenager.

Jyotsna and Samar did not discuss their relationship again during his remaining days in Tezpur. On the last day, Samar held and hugged his baby girl as tears rolled down his cheeks. Jyotsna was crying, too. Samar left for the airport with a heavy heart.

Perhaps it was time to wait and hope for the best…

***

CHAPTER 28

Three months had passed since Samar visited Tezpur. It was a lonely, heavy, and disappointing time for him. Hopes of reconciliation with Jyotsna faded with time. He tried to raise the subject of her return now and then, but she avoided any direct response. If pursued further, she pressed for some more time to decide.

Samar missed Jyotsna and his baby girl. Video calling seemed the only option left to see and connect with them. It became an important part of his daily routine, something he never missed, come what may! The baby girl responded to his calls. She recognized her name when he called out to her. Samar, during his last visit, had suggested the name 'Avni', meaning Mother Earth. Everyone loved it.

In Tezpur, Jyotsna's daily routine revolved around Avni. It was exhausting yet satisfying. Every now and then, she pondered the serious conversation she had with Samar that night. She noticed the changes in him. He became responsive and responsible as a father. He was regular in calling them and dropped hints about missing them. He ordered baby apparel, diapers, baby milk products, etc., to be delivered to the Dekas' address.

Jyotsna was aware of Samar's internal turmoil. He pretended to be happy, but his eyes looked despondent, as if he was no longer hopeful. Mrs Barua often remarked during phone calls, "When are you coming back, Jyotsna? Your husband seems sad. He misses you and Avni."

Jyotsna was also restive. Although the change in Samar was encouraging, she still had apprehensions that prevented her from thinking clearly and positively about their future. She toyed with the idea of doing research work at Tezpur Central University itself and fending for herself and Avni. There were marital offers for Meghna. The Dekas were keen to arrive at an early decision. Sometimes, she felt like an outsider at her maternal home, like other married women who visited their mother's home for a brief stay but longed to return to their husband. She could understand the hidden meaning behind seemingly innocent comments from neighbourhood aunties who prodded, "All well? When are you going back to Delhi?"

If she went back to Delhi, would things improve?

Would Samar devote himself completely to her and Avni? Would they regain happiness and marital bliss?

***

It was an unusually bright and sunny Saturday afternoon in the third week of January. Samar woke up from his afternoon siesta, threw a red Naga shawl over his shoulders, and made his way to the kitchen. He brewed a cup of coffee and dialled Jyotsna's number for a regular call. Her phone was out of the coverage area. He sipped his coffee and picked up a monthly current affairs magazine. After about 15 minutes, he dialled again, but he could still not reach her phone.

Forty minutes after another failed call, he called Meghna again, but got the same response. He then called up his father-in-law, who picked up on the second ring.

"Jyotsna and Meghna have gone to the market. There must be a network connectivity issue. Don't worry, I will ask her to call you back when she returns."

Samar was disappointed. He was eager to see Avni and now had to wait till their return. Dr Deka owned a basic mobile, so a video call was not possible. Samar switched on the TV and whiled away the time, surfing channels, waiting for a call from Jyotsna.

The loud ring of the doorbell startled Samar. He had dozed off on the sofa and was not expecting anyone. He glanced at the wall clock. It was ten minutes past 7 pm. It was unusual that Jyotsna had not called him until now.

He opened the door and stood stunned. Avni, dressed in a fuchsia pink fancy frock, red stockings, and a dark pink jacket, was in a stroller at the doorstep!

Was this real?

Avni was gazing at him, eyes beaming and bright.

Samar knelt in front of the stroller. Tears rolled down his face as he took Avni's hands and kissed them.

"Is Daddy home?"

Jyotsna was on the stairs purposely to conceal herself from view. Meghna was standing behind her.

Samar picked up Avni and hugged her, laughing and crying at the same time. Jyotsna joined him as he extended his arm towards her. She pinched his warm, wet cheeks and patted his back.

"Why didn't you tell me? I would have picked you up from Tezpur or at least from the airport!"

"Oh! Your daughter wanted to surprise you, Daddy."

"Throughout the afternoon today, I was wondering why you were not picking up my calls."

"We were taking a ride in the sky, Daddy!"

Avni was looking continuously at Samar. She had long, beautiful eyelashes like her mother.

***

EPILOGUE

Abha applied for adoption before the Child Welfare Committee. The CWC initially had reservations about Abha being a single parent. The DM sent a written recommendation to the CWC on Samar's request to consider the case. The recommendation yielded the desired results. The CWC granted her adoption.

Abha shifted to the flat on the Noida Expressway. She enrolled Roshni in a well-known school in Noida. She started working as a schoolteacher in a prominent school in Noida. She had a busy schedule, tending to Roshni, dropping her off, and picking her up from school every day, but she enjoyed it thoroughly. Roshni called her 'Mamma'. Abha changed her mobile number and other contact details so that no one from her past could contact her, including Samar.

Jyotsna submitted a project to the Department of Biotechnology under the Ministry of Science and Technology. The DBT approved her project and funded it for two years. Jyotsna joined Professor Rajanna's laboratory at the South Campus.

Samar bought a new hatchback on loan. Jyotsna commuted by it. They hired a live-in nanny to attend to Avni. Despite a heavy workload, Samar started coming home as soon as possible in the evenings, with Avni being the motivating factor.

Avni started crawling. She also started to speak some words, Samar's favourite being '*Dedda*', her version of Daddy!

***